Through the Oval Lens

Through the Oval Lens

Gregory Kieler

Through the Oval Lens

Published by Concise Prose, LLC
Brooksville, FL
conciseprose.com

Published 2021
First Addition

ISBN 978-0-578-94577-4
Edited by Christopher D Kieler

For the woman that saved me,

and my four listeners,

Michael,
Ben,
Chris,
& John

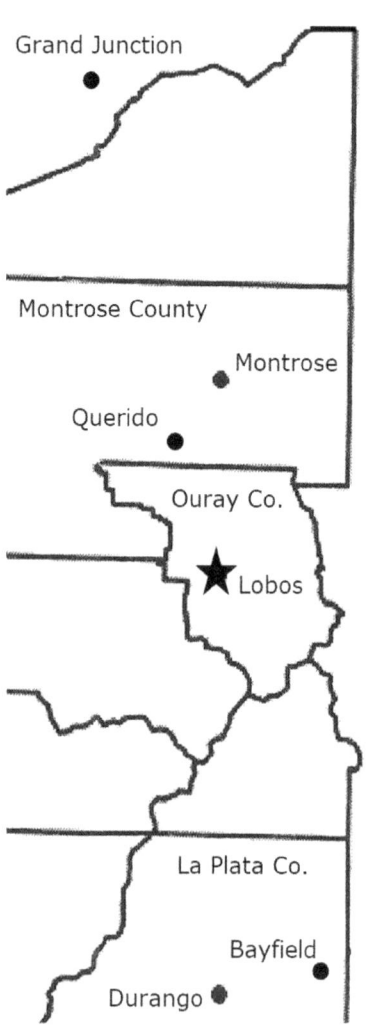

Grand Junction

Montrose County

Montrose

Querido

Ouray Co.

Lobos

La Plata Co.

Bayfield

Durango

N

W   E

S

San Juan
Mountain Range
Southwest Colorado

Scale of Miles

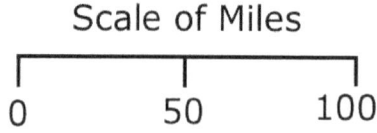

0   50   100

Contents

Chapter 1

Born Flatlander

It was the *fourteener* that drew Dalton to Horse Head Trail, a fourteen-thousand-foot summit. He had already hiked nearly as high. All the peaks surrounding his new Colorado home exceeded eleven, the highest more than twelve. But God had only made so many fourteeners, and relatively few people had ever climbed them.

Just inside the trailhead, the path sloped gently upward, tracing a glacial stream, its soft gurgle providing a soothing soundtrack to the hike. The winding creek banks were lined with pines and firs, the surrounding hills and meadows covered in Aspens. Intermittent whispers from the conifers descended on the trail as warmed valley air pushed up the mountain between their slender branches and needles.

The trail would ascend twenty-five-hundred feet in the first three miles. The creek's water flow was certain to become a rush, and then a roar, as it charged down the steep grade that lay ahead. The converging lines on Dalton's topographical map guaranteed it. But two miles in, the path remained tame. The stream's resonance remained a gentle murmur as it traversed its bed of rock.

The creek turned sharply around an enormous boulder. The behemoth partially blocked the trail. A clearing above the fallen rock suggested a recent slide, the flattened trees exposing a descending mountain ridge, dictating the stream's course. As Dalton skirted the obstacle and rounded the bend, the acoustics of the waterflow finally changed. A faint chain of variously-toned disjointed pulses filled the air. The peculiar noise grew louder the further Dalton hiked, but the trail remained inexplicably flat.

A pounding beat of acoustic explosions drummed in Dalton's ears as the path once again turned and the stream revealed its secret. A magnificent waterfall plunged to a boulder-strewn bed. Dense vapor hovered above the basin as the torrent crashed unceasingly onto the rock. Below the falls, a vine of micro-tributaries re-gathered the water, reconstituting the stream.

A wisp of wind delivered a refreshing spritz to Dalton's face. He moved deeper into the mist, breathing in the damp air until he stood beside the towering cascade and its thundering cacophony. He rested several minutes, then pulled out his laminated topographical map. *"It seems, I may have read this thing wrong,"* he thought, grinning. *"Now, how do I get up this bad boy?"*

The answer was only yards away. The trail led directly to the base of the falls, disappearing behind the wall of water. Dalton emerged from the damp passage to an ascent of enormous elevation and pitch, a virtual staircase of zigzagging turns, *switchbacks*. He had read horror stories about the radically-winding trails but had never traversed one. Each step of the trek added nearly a foot of elevation. Every few yards the trail reversed course, placing him several feet above where he'd been. By the third switch, Dalton's quads were screaming. The fatigue caused him to misstep, jamming his boot-toe into a boulder, gliding his knee into a sharp stone. He stopped to inspect the abrasion, a superficial wound. He turned to glimpse the elevation behind him, but the thick foliage deprived him of the gratification.

Dalton pushed through the fourth, fifth, and sixth switchbacks. His respiration was heavy and sweat streamed from his brow. He paused again, wiping away the perspiration. He took a long drink from his water bottle. He was determined to reach the top without stopping. His heart pounded like the water crashing on the rocks below. He struck out in a slow and steady pace through the twists and turns of the trail. As he rounded the fourteenth switch, he found the relief he was looking for.

The trail crossed the water near the falls' mouth. The stream was wide and once again tame, revealing stride-spaced boulders, bank to bank. Dalton stopped midstream; his feet planted firmly on two flat, dry rocks. Water rushed between his straddled legs and disappeared over the precipice into the vapor cloud. He crept closer to the cliff's edge until he could see the base of the switchbacks. He pitched a small stone between the trees. Seconds later, the rock splashed into the shallow pool below.

Dalton guzzled the last of his water. He bent down, submerging the bottle in the stream, quickly refilling it. He turned and looked up the trail. The tree line wasn't far off, and he could see the barren fourteen-thousand-foot peak above it. The path traced a wide wooded valley situated between two lesser mountains, like shoulders below the monster's head. There would be many more switchbacks, but for now, the way was flat and straight.

Farther along the trail and finally out of earshot of the falls, Dalton's eye was drawn to a mining camp ruin in a rocky outcrop near the valley's edge. Among the debris outside the boarded-up shaft lay a rusted sign bent down in the weeds.

Winning Stakes Mining Co. - Site #14

Dalton considered the challenges the workers would have had bringing equipment up the falls. *"How in the world did they get up here?"* he thought. A second idea revealed a dangerous impulse. *"Could be worth a closer look on the way back."*

The trail continued to trace the now gently flowing stream through a green meadow marked with wildflowers. Dalton took in the fragrance of the vegetation and watched bees busily collect pollen. At last, he saw the source of the stream that had been his guide. Nestled at the far end of the meadow, lay a lake. Feeding it, the last of the winter snows and small glaciers melting from the surrounding peaks.

As Dalton approached the lake, he saw a fisherman on the near shore repeatedly rolling his line across the water's surface. The trail passed within twenty feet of the angler. The fisherman appeared to be a young man, about Dalton's age. "Catching anything?" Dalton asked.

"Not yet, but I can see brookies," the angler replied. "I've caught Lake Trout here, too."

Dalton understood by *brookies*, the fisherman meant Brook Trout. "You eat them or let them go?" he asked. The thought of warm fish made his mouth water.

"Sometimes I'll eat a brookie, but I release the rest," the fisherman said. "At least until I catch a Lake Trout big enough to put on the wall."

Dalton immediately liked the stranger and offered a friendly challenge, "I'll be back this way in a couple of hours," he said. "If you catch a couple, I'll cook them for us."

"Sounds good," the young man responded. "Where you headed?"

"Summit," Dalton replied.

The fisherman looked up the trail that would be Dalton's path. "Ambitious," he said. "It's beautiful up there."

Dalton Wallace never dreamed he'd live in the mountains. Before his family moved to Colorado, he'd never even been out of the Midwest. An attractive kid with sandy brown hair, his physique was proportional and athletic. His blue eyes and bushy eyebrows were set in a round, friendly face. His average-size nose sloped through a smattering of freckles to a pleasantly cleft ball. His build suited him for golf or tennis, but his life circumstances hadn't allowed for country club style recreation.

Dalton wished the fisherman good luck and turned up the trail.

The path traced the lake shore to a steep diagonal run between the fourteener and its more prominent shoulder. Patches of snow and ice glistened as the noon sun hammered away at the last of their winter realm. At last, Dalton could see the altitudinal tree line in all directions, a practical panoramic no-grow barrier to vegetative life. It was the first time he'd seen one from above. He crossed a narrow ridge between the two mountains, leaving the smaller peak and alpine lake behind.

The trail turned sharply, and Dalton again spotted the crest of the fourteener. The way to the summit lay completely exposed, the terrain mere rock and soil. A chain of switchbacks zigzagged the naked monster leading to a straight run to the summit.

At thirteen thousand-five hundred feet and the switchbacks behind him, Dalton's aerobic pace was strenuous but comfortable in the thin air. The impending final ascent made him exuberant. He was already higher than he'd ever climbed, and he was about to summit a height most would never have the opportunity to try. Time slowed in a way usually reserved for hardship. He was in the moment like never before.

A hundred feet from his goal, exertion-derived endorphins surged through Dalton's brain; euphoric waves awoke realms of emotion and spirit within him he'd never felt before.

As he reached the summit, Dalton took in the spectacular view and pondered his accomplishment. Mountains strung out in every direction. The lake below appeared little more than a puddle, its flow to the falls imperceptible. Water streamed from his eyes. He felt small, yet infinitely valued. A sense of mystical gratitude overcame him that he reasoned was, itself, a gift.

With memories captured in his mind and cell phone, Dalton hiked down the mountain. Approaching the meadow, he again spotted the young angler, still fishing the lake, but on the opposite side from the trail. It would be a longer hike, but Dalton's hunger and interest in getting to know someone his age drove him. "*Hopefully, he's had some luck,*" he thought.

Dalton had made his way around the lake and was about to shout out a greeting when the fisherman turned and raised a stringer of trout. "*Excellent,*" Dalton thought, lifting a thumb up. By the time he arrived, the angler had already assembled a fire-ring out of stones.

"I'm Jacob," the stranger said.

Jacob Burrell was a born mountain man. Raised in southwestern Colorado, he grew up fishing and hunting. Blond-haired and with average height, he had a muscular build that frequently provoked questions about weightlifting. He'd never picked one up. Jacob's strenuous hobbies contributed to his physique, but it was largely genetic. His father had played linebacker for Colorado State.

Dalton introduced himself, reaching out for a fist bump.

The two squatted side-by-side cleaning the trout on the bank. Dalton followed Jacob's lead, removing the fish's guts and heads. They gathered material for a fire, leaves and tree bark for starter, twigs for kindling. Dalton found a dead tree, succumbed to erosion on the steep bank. He broke off a limb with a strong kick and partitioned it with several more blows. Within minutes, the fire was raging.

As the voluntary chef, Dalton planned to cook the fish on skewers. He looked for green branches to cut, but his new friend had another idea.

"Hold on a minute," Jacob said. He pulled out a small roll of tinfoil and a zipper bag full of spices. He rinsed the catch a final time and sprinkled on the mix. Wrapping each fish individually in foil, he placed the rolls on top of the fire's hot coals. "In ten minutes, we'll be eating," he said.

"You were ready," Dalton said, "but I was supposed to cook."

"Don't worry about it," Jacob replied.

Dalton was sure fish had never tasted so good. When they'd finished eating, he stood up. "At least let me do the dishes," he exclaimed. He scooped up the scraps of foil, making a tight ball of them, and slid the waste into his jeans' pocket.

Jacob laughed.

Dalton and Jacob quickly learned that the bigger coincidence was not meeting at altitude, but that they hadn't met in town. They both lived in the small, nearby town of Lobos.

"So, you moved into the Tucker place," Jacob said.

Dalton nodded, affirmatively.

"Well, you make four of us in town, then," Jacob said. "You, me, Jimmy Irwin, and Ben Childress, when he gets back——. If he gets back."

Dalton looked at Jacob, puzzled.

Jacob tried to clarify. "Ben's a friend, our age," he said. "His parents are divorced. He moves back and forth between his mom in town and his grandparents' place over in Montrose, near school. His dad's out in California. I guess his pops didn't bring him back after a visit this summer. The cops are looking for them."

Dalton looked down, thinking of the kid and his family. "Well, I have to go," he said, noticing the time. "My dad's picking me up at the trailhead in a couple of hours."

"I'll probably fish another hour or so," Jacob replied. "How about another hike tomorrow, close to town?"

Chapter 2

Lobos

The wake-up call blaring from Dalton's wristwatch was having no effect. He simply wasn't budging.

Steve Wallace rose early and heard his son's alarm. He dressed quietly, leaving his wife to her slumber. He wondered why his son wanted up early and gently tapped his shoulder. "Hey, are you getting up?" he said.

Dalton wiped the sleep from his eyes, snatching his beeping watch from the nightstand. "Eight o'clock," he said, groggily. "Maybe I'll sleep a bit longer."

"Nope, seven," Steve teased with a juvenile grin on his face. "We're in mountain time zone. You still need to adjust your watch. Hey, your mom and I saw a little store downtown. If they're open, I'll buy us some breakfast. I need a cup of coffee."

"I'm getting up," Dalton said. "Just let me get a shower."

Dalton's bedroom was located on the second floor of their new home, where an oversized front window offered generous perspectives of the Lobos valley and adjacent mountains. A large windowsill provided a comfortable place to sit. The nineteenth-century wood-framed home sat on the elevated edge of the valley, atop a foundation of granite boulders. The rock reflected the color of the local mountain stone and was organized like a mortar-bound jigsaw puzzle. The house's underpinning literally backed into the slope of the mountain, giving the appearance that the foundation was taller in the front than the back. The house's relative elevation, and Dalton's second-story bedroom, lifted the views from his window above the trees, homes, and buildings of the valley.

Dalton sat on the windowsill, sliding clean socks over his freshly scrubbed feet. As a jay bird chirped outside the open window, a cool breeze sifted through the surrounding trees, filling the room with the fragrance of mountain pine. Dalton tied his shoes and stood to take in the crystal-clear morning.

On the adjacent mountain, vast green swaths of spruce and firs jutted up from the valley in wide strokes, tapering toward the tree line. Strings of Aspens wove their way through the forest, their green leaves offering no hint of the golden lace they'd resemble in the fall. Sheer rock faces and heaps of fallen stone sporadically interrupted the woodland. Small patches of snow and glacial ice punctuated the subalpine scene above the trees.

As Dalton scanned the mountainside, his eye was drawn to a group of crumbling structures. A dilapidated waterwheel stood halfcocked next to a glacier-fed stream, many of its paddles fallen away. A few outbuildings stood nearby in various states of repair. Among the ruins, lay a large, partially-barricaded opening in the mountain. Dalton recalled the mining camp he'd observed off Horse Head Trail the previous day and noted the similarities between the two complexes.

A whistle Dalton recognized as his father's permeated the room through the open window, though Steve was nowhere in sight. Dalton moved across the corner of his room to a side-window, facing down the street toward the town center.

Steve saw Dalton and signaled he was heading downtown.

Dalton observed how several buildings in the business district backed into the mountain in the same manner as his home, though several cleared lots separated his house from the first building.

The entire town of Lobos filled a valley floor less than a quarter-mile wide and a mile long. A half dozen downtown structures lay distributed on both sides of the main street; some shared dividing walls and were connected outside by wooden walkways. Dalton could see that a couple of the buildings had relatively updated windows and doors, but he imagined most of the structures were more than a hundred years old. The rest of the valley consisted of a few dozen houses and small ranches. A smattering of farm buildings sat in narrow pastures on the town's margins.

Dalton caught up to his dad at Breitling's Grocery.

Steve was happy to find the store open and filled with the aroma of fresh coffee. He spied the pot near the front corner of the store. The register counter partially obstructed the condiment bar and Steve couldn't decide if it was self-serve or not. There was no one to ask. He was pondering the repercussions of helping himself when a short round man with dyed black hair appeared from the back room.

"Can I help you?" the shopkeeper asked.

"Medium coffee, please," Steve replied.

"It's self-serve, but I'd be happy to pour you a cup," the grocer offered.

Steve shrugged unnoticeably about the confusion. He surmised from the shopkeeper's peppy attitude the man had already had his coffee. "That would be nice of you," he said.

"Are you the family that moved into the Tucker place?" the pudgy fellow asked.

"That's us," Steve said. "We just got into town a few weeks ago. I'm Steve Wallace, and this is my son, Dalton." The younger Wallace had just pulled up alongside his dad. Steve nodded toward his son who was placing a package of chocolate doughnuts and a bottle of orange juice on the counter.

The man didn't manage a look at Dalton. He snapped the plastic lid on the foam cup and placed the coffee in front of Steve. "Well, welcome to town," he said.

Dalton noticed the shopkeeper's omission toward him but had little concern; he knew some adults showed more consideration toward young people than others.

"Thanks," Steve said, handing the man a five-dollar bill. He'd also noticed the man's slight toward his son but didn't think much of it, seeing as it hadn't appeared to bother Dalton. "Well, I guess we'll be seeing a lot of each other," Steve said, "assuming this coffee tastes as good as it smells, that is. What's your name, sir?"

"Max Breitling," he replied. "We're open Monday through Friday, seven-to-five, Saturdays till noon. We live in town, though, if you need anything after hours. We're the only two-story house on this block."

Breitling's Grocery was the best thing to happen to Lobos in decades. Before Max and his wife set-up shop a year earlier, folks in town had to drive many miles for as little as a gallon of milk. The lack of services in town wasn't without cause. The sparse population of the region, and relatively meager local incomes, made making a living in retail in Lobos difficult. Steve was happy to find Breitling's in town, even if the impressive inventory and long store hours seemed hard to justify.

"Great," Steve said. "Thanks again for the coffee." He took his change from the shopkeeper.

As Steve led Dalton toward the exit, he saw a half-empty newspaper rack next to the door. "Let me take a paper too," he said, turning back to Breitling.

"All we have is the Montrose Gazette, just arrived," Breitling replied. "The Post won't be here for another hour or so. We're a long way from Denver."

"This one's fine," Steve said, handing over the money.

Steve and Dalton exited the shop to the wooden sidewalk.

Steve paused and took a sip of his coffee as he scanned the front page of the newspaper. Halfway down the sheet, he read a startling headline.

Lobos Youth Missing

Steve instantly tensed-up. "Dalton, hold on a minute," he said. "I need to read something."

The headline could have been from the Kansas City Star. Steve thought they'd left that kind of nonsense behind. As far as he was concerned, the premier fringe-benefit of moving to Colorado was the fact that it was rural. The fewer the people, the fewer the problems. The endless wilderness surrounding Lobos would keep his son busy with mountain recreation. The intrinsic dangers therein, God could handle.

Dalton leaned against an awning post. He was already enjoying his doughnuts, gazing up at the old mining camp.

Steve spread out his newspaper on a wooden barrel placed on the street. As he read the article, he grew frustrated. The piece was less than comprehensive. At least the information given was encouraging. The Childress case was considered domestic in nature, a type of dispute that generally ended quickly, and rarely with violence.

Steve looked up from his newspaper. His coffee had cooled some. He took a long swig. Folding the paper, he moved to his son.

"What's in the news?" Dalton asked.

"Not much, as it turns out," Steve said. "Saturday papers are usually pretty thin." He made a mental note to stop back later for the Denver Post.

From where they stood on the street, Dalton and his dad could see the entire business district of Lobos. Behind Breitling's Grocery stood a farm implement dealer, its inventory yard taking up most of the rest of the block. Steve noted a two-story house behind the grocery store, the Breitling residence. The only other commercial building on Breitling's side of Main stood on the corner of the adjacent block. The structure lacked any type of store front, and its entrance faced the side street. The faded letters above the door could barely be made out.

SHERIFF'S ANNEX

Three buildings stood on the opposite side of the main drive, all two-story homes converted into retail shops. Each house backed into the mountain in the manner of Dalton's home, a couple hundred yards down the valley. Two of the structures displayed *For Rent* placards in their windows and appeared unoccupied. The third building had a small sign taped to the inside of a makeshift display window.

ANTIQUES

An additional illuminated sign hung inside the antique store's showroom indicating the store was open.

"Let's check it out," Dalton said.

Lit sign or not, Steve noted the dark showroom and assumed the shop was closed. But since they were in no particular hurry, he agreed to take a look.

As they crossed the street, Dalton noticed the remnants of other house foundations along the base of the mountain between the antique shop and their new home. He tried to count how many houses had once been there, but most of the rock used for the underpinnings had been hauled away or repurposed.

The antique store was closed as Steve expected. Dalton pressed his nose to the glass. A light in the stairwell leading to a second floor was illuminated. He considered someone might live there. The main floor was filled with furniture, trunks, rugs, and other old things Dalton didn't recognize. Finally, he noticed a glass case with a hand-written sign indicating the store offered coins for sale. "*At last, something interesting,*" he thought.

Steve interrupted Dalton's mental scavenger hunt. "Let me grab a coffee refill and let's head home," he said. "Your mother's probably up and wondering where we are."

As Steve walked out of Breitling's with his freshly filled cup, he found Dalton gazing down the mountain ridge toward their home.

Dalton suggested they walk back on the opposite side of the street along the mountain. He wanted to take a closer look at the other two, yet uninvestigated commercial buildings up for rent, and the remnants of the houses strewn between the commercial district and their home. Before they crossed, Dalton and his dad walked directly in front of the Sheriff's Annex. While they'd been distracted at the antique store, a police cruiser had pulled in.

The car was unoccupied. The annex door was ajar. As they passed by, a deep voice permeated the opening and echoed onto the street. A uniformed officer was visible inside. He was speaking sternly to a person hidden from view.

Dalton couldn't understand what was being said, but from the man's tone it was clear; the officer was not pleased. Not wanting to appear nosey, Steve kept his pace, leading Dalton quickly past the annex. When they were out of earshot of the building, Dalton spoke. "I guess that's an actual sheriff's office," he said. "I wonder what's going on."

"Not sure," Steve replied, "but it's good to be on the right side of the law."

"Definitely," Dalton offered in reply, gazing across the valley at the adjacent mountain. "You know, there's an old mine up there." He was pointing spiritedly at the crumbling camp. "Do you think there's still silver or gold?"

"Off limits, son," Steve said curtly.

The point was well-taken. Still, Dalton couldn't help thinking about what might have been left behind by the old miners.

Chapter 3

Cheyanne Connery

After an intense afternoon hike with his new friend, Jacob, Dalton was hungry. "Mom, Dad," he said, "let's order pizza."

The realization dawned on all of them simultaneously; there wasn't going to be any pizza delivery to their tiny and remote town.

"Montrose," Dalton said, finally. "Let's drive."

Montrose was a much larger town, and relatively close by. Both of Dalton's parents' new employers were based there, as well as Dalton's future school and the family's new church.

Susan finally weighed in on Dalton's dinner idea. "I think it's a great plan," she said. "What do you think, Steve?"

"I'm in," he replied.

As the family headed north toward Montrose, Steve saw a familiar sign for another town, Querido. He was thinking about shortening the evening's drive and slowed to make the turn. "Let's check it out," he said. "I've driven through before. I think there's a couple of restaurants. Maybe we'll get lucky and find a good one. It's a cut-through to Montrose, anyway."

Querido wasn't much bigger than Lobos but featured a relatively modern downtown. Surprisingly for the late hour, several restaurants and shops appeared open.

Dalton spotted the pizzeria first. "Look, right there," he exclaimed. "And it must be good too, look at all the cars."

Steve Wallace pulled into an open parking spot near the restaurant. There was a wait for a table, so they put their name in with the hostess. From his vantage point in the lobby, Dalton observed a distinguished looking man in cowboy-boots walking around the dining room, smiling, chatting with guests. Dalton assumed he was the owner. A young couple with two small children in strollers made their way toward the exit. Dalton stood and held the door for them.

Susan saw the servers cleaning a table and she suspected they'd be seated ahead of the projected wait-time. The tempting aroma in the restaurant fueled Dalton's hunger. The hostess called their name and led the Wallaces to the dining room.

A young waitress promptly brought set-ups and menus. "Hi," she said, "my name is Cheyanne. I'll be your server."

Dalton was instantly smitten. Cheyanne was the most beautiful girl he'd ever seen. It was as if he were hypnotized; he simply couldn't take his eyes off the young lady. He was still pulling himself together when the waitress addressed him.

"What would you like to drink?" Cheyanne asked.

Dalton hesitated. He simply couldn't pull the trigger. Susan could see Dalton was stymied and came to his rescue. "A cola and two un-sweet teas," she said. "Can we also get water for the table and three dinner salads; two Italian and one Ranch?"

"Of course," the waitress replied.

Cheyanne Connery had noticed the young man's reaction, but she was used to it. Her long auburn hair and striking green eyes caught the attention of most boys. She was self-assured for her age, if impetuous. Her confidence was not surprising, considering her upbringing. Her entrepreneur parents had nurtured Cheyanne's talents and encouraged her aspirations, but sometimes their daughter left them cringing with her impulsive judgements. Owning a family restaurant required long hours and hard work from the entire family. Cheyanne managed her part, even as she maintained good grades, played soccer, and cheered.

Susan looked intently at the young waitress. "Excuse me for asking," she said. "You look so young. Are you old enough to work as a waitress? I mean, legally."

"That's all-right mam, I'm fifteen, sixteen in a couple of months," she said. "That's old enough to work in a restaurant in Colorado. But I've been helping-out since I was tall enough to reach the sink. This is my folks' place."

"Well, your family has a lovely restaurant," Steve interjected. "We'll also take a large pizza with the works."

"Thanks," Cheyanne said, smiling, "I'll put your order in and bring your drinks and salads."

The young waitress made eye contact with each of them before returning to the kitchen. Dalton wasn't sure, but he thought the girl's gaze had held an extra second on him. "*Shocking*," he thought, certain the waitress had noticed his nervous behavior.

Steve and Susan observed their son across the table, seemingly frozen, staring at the doorway where Cheyanne had disappeared. The kitchen door swung closed. Dalton's mouth was slightly ajar.

C heyanne passed the Wallace's order to the cooks and moved to the beverage fountain to pour their drinks.

Another waitress, an older lady, stood behind her. "That's a handsome young man at table twelve," she said. "You know him?"

"No," Cheyanne said. "Probably tourists, passing through."

"He's a little old to be vacationing with mommy and daddy," the woman said.

"Either way, don't know him," Cheyanne said. She placed the last of the filled glasses on her tray and hoisted it above her shoulder.

The older waitress leaned over, sneaking a peak at the Wallace's table through a round port in the kitchen door. "Well, he's still looking this way," she said.

Cheyanne slid toward the window, one eye breaking the plain. "He's cute," she conceded. "But he's probably just another little boy with whiskers." She bumped the door open with her hip and carried the drinks out.

Chapter 4

Winning Stakes

Winning Stakes Mining Company; Dalton typed the name he'd read on the beat-up sign near Horse Head Trail into his laptop. He couldn't remember the claim's site number. Hundreds of links instantly queued up.

Winning Stakes was a defunct mining conglomerate, formerly based in Colorado Springs. At one time, the company had mines all over the western United States and Canada. After sifting through several websites, Dalton found a list of operations, including several in southwestern Colorado, two in his own county of Ouray. No doubt, he had seen one of them earlier that week off Horse Head Trail. He had a hunch the other one was visible from his bedroom window, high above Lobos.

Dalton was seated at the kitchen table. His mother sat across from him, ostensibly sorting the snail mail. Despite Dalton's attempt to concentrate, Susan continued to ask him questions: How was he spending his days while she and Steve were away at work? How was his new friend, Jacob? Dalton casually mentioned the abandoned mining camp he'd observed on his way up Horse Head Trail.

"Well, I hope you had the good sense to stay away from it," Susan said, tensing up.

"Yes, Mother," Dalton replied, "I'm not stupid, you know."

Susan realized she'd come on too strong, should have given Dalton the benefit of the doubt. "Of course, you're not," she said.

Dalton adjusted his computer screen and squared up solidly behind it. He augmented his search: *Winning Stakes Mining Company Ouray County Colorado.*

Dozens of links from a narrow date range, years earlier, instantly appeared on his screen. News archives, mostly. None of which having anything to do with mining precious metals.

The lead-ins were shocking. Dalton clicked on an article from the Denver Post. A fugitive had been killed by a sheriff near a Winning Stakes mine facility in Ouray County, Colorado. The deceased criminal had been involved in a home invasion and robbery in Denver. The victims had included a wealthy businessman. A fortune in silver coins had been stolen. There had been two assailants. The man and his wife had been tied up at gunpoint and surrendered the contents of a home safe to save their lives. Denver neighbors reported seeing an early model Chevrolet with Arizona plates in the area.

"*Those people are lucky to be alive,*" Dalton thought. He briefly looked up from his screen. Susan had left the room.

Dalton read additional articles about the incident. The slain thief had surfaced in Lobos, Colorado. The Ouray County Sheriff had observed a car matching the report parked behind a local grocery store.

"*Breitling's,*" Dalton thought.

As the sheriff surveilled the vehicle, he observed a man emerging from a trailhead off the mountain. The man entered the sought-after car. As the sheriff approached, he found the door open, and the fugitive seated behind the steering wheel. The suspect raised a gun, and the lawman emptied his service revolver. The man died at the scene.

After the incident, a massive search of the local mountains and abandoned Winning Stakes mine complex took place, led by Deputy Thero Buford, a recent transfer from La Plata County. The accomplice to the home invasion and robbery was never found. Nor was the fortune in silver.

Dalton was struck by the irony of the crook's flight from the crime scene, "*This guy must have been a real genius,*" he thought. "*He drives for four hours, then parks next to a sheriff's office.*"

Chapter 5

The Hunt

Dalton received two presents for his sixteenth birthday from his parents: A twenty-two caliber rifle, and a certificate for a safety-training course. Jacob had the same gun model, though his rifle was noticeably worn. He took the training with Dalton, anyway. It was a chance for the two of them to visit the sports store in Montrose.

Jacob's long family history in Ouray County had led to numerous friendships with area ranchers; Jacob and his dad had hunting privileges on most of the local lands. Mr. Burrell was especially close to a local rancher, Mack Halstead. Jacob also helped-out occasionally on the man's operation when an extra hand was needed. Halstead paid him well, and Jacob was allowed the run of the place, year-round.

Dalton and Jacob hiked toward a valley near the back of Halstead's ranch. The path was kept clear by cattle, but a pair of deep, wheel-spaced ruts suggested the route had been used for generations. Rotting, unstrung fence posts loosely traced the road.

Jacob spotted a rusty street sign in the distance, nailed to a dead tree. "There's our first target," he said, picking up the pace.

Even at a distance, Dalton could see dozens of bullet holes in the old sign. "Looks like we won't be the first," he said.

Jacob acknowledged many of the piercings were on his account. He stopped a reasonable distance from the target. "Watch this," he said. He armed his weapon and sounded off ten consecutive clinks through the old sign.

Dalton had been a good shot with his pellet gun back in Kansas. He quickly discovered his talent extended to his twenty-two rifle. "Let me try," he said. He loaded his weapon and matched Jacob's feat, banging out ten out of ten.

As they walked toward the bullet-riddled shield, Dalton paced off the space, estimating the distance. "About fifty feet," he said.

The pair finished their hike to the valley and attempted to set-up a more challenging target. Jacob found a metal snuff lid lying on the ground and propped it up on the side of a hill. Feeling confident, he paced off ninety feet and drew a line in the dirt with his boot. "Let's have a contest," he challenged. "You go first."

Dalton obliged. He loaded the maximum ten bullets into his gun magazine and slid the clip into the rifle. He placed the gunstock firmly against his shoulder. He visually placed the metal pin of the gun's open sights on the target, adjusting the barrel vertically and horizontally until the pin nestled in the center of the u-shaped rear sight. He released the gun's safety. Dalton grew still; the beating of his heart and respiration grew loud in his ears. He rhythmically squeezed the trigger at the bottom of each breath until the rifle was empty.

Jacob had been scanning the hillside for any sign of impact. "You missed by a mile," he said. "I didn't see a bit of dust fly."

"I don't think so," Dalton said. "Let's check the target before you shoot." He disabled his weapon and walked over to the snuff lid. Jacob followed. The pounding of the rounds had driven the lid's tin rim into the earth like a plug. The shiny sphere sported ten holes, tightly grouped near its center.

"I can't beat that," Jacob conceded.

Deer season was approaching. It would be the first big-game hunt in Dalton's life. While he was allowed, as a sixteen-year-old, to use his rifle to hunt small-game, he would need an adult along to hunt deer. For Jacob, hunting was an annual affair, something he'd done with his dad since he was eleven. He had taken a deer in five consecutive seasons. Fortunately for Dalton, Mr. Burrell had offered to let him join in on their hunt and serve as his mentor.

The small, twenty-two caliber rifles Dalton and Jacob trained with were perfectly suited to their hobby. The light ammunition was easy on their ears, and their wallets. But a high-powered weapon would be needed to take down a deer. For his part, Jacob was all set. He had the pick of several guns his father owned. Dalton had been looking for a good, used rifle ever since they started talking about the hunt, but with little luck. It wasn't that there weren't any good guns around. The problem was finding one at an affordable price. Shopping online had become part of his daily routine.

Dalton woke before his alarm. The dim light in his bedroom told him it was overcast, and a clap of thunder confirmed it. Soon, large raindrops were battering the roof above his bed. He rolled out of the sack, brushed his teeth, and threw on his clothing before heading downstairs. His folks had long left for work. As he slurped his cereal, Dalton scrolled through the sporting section of a local trading website. "Nothing, as usual," he muttered. He gazed out the kitchen window toward the town center. The rain obscured his view.

Turning back to his computer, Dalton scanned the menu of product categories on the trading site. *"Pets are always interesting,"* he thought. As he attempted to click on the category, it was clear his superior marksmanship with his twenty-two-rifle failed to translate to a mouse. He was immediately directed to the *Personals* section of the online marketplace. Horrified, he scrambled to redirect the computer. But before he could make the jump, he noticed a listing prominently positioned near the top of the query: *Browning A-Bolt Rifle w/Scope - $400*. The peculiar circumstances of finding the gun were instantly irrelevant. Dalton was sure he'd found the perfect rifle for the hunt. "That's it," he cried out in the empty house.

Dalton quickly scrolled to *Male Life Giver* in his contacts and clicked on his dad's cell number. "I found it, Dad," he said, "a Browning for $400. It was on the local swap-site, in the *Personals* section."

Steve was at his Montrose office. *"Personals?* Were you looking for a date?" he joked.

"It was a misfire," he said, "but there it was, a Browning A-Bolt with a mounted scope. The ad says it's like new. It sounds perfect."

"Interesting," Steve said.

"I can't un-see what else was on that page, by the way," Dalton said.

The Browning model had been first on Dalton's wish list. This version was bored for a 300 Winchester Magnum cartridge, more than enough load to take down a deer. With a powerful scope and accurate marksmanship, the A-Bolt would be lethal for hundreds of yards.

The description and price Dalton described sounded good to Steve. He knew his son needed a hunting rifle. He and Susan had agreed their son would get one when they found the right deal. They'd been budgeting for it, and Steve thought this might be a winner. He took the number from Dalton and hung up.

The sequence of the phone numbers indicated a Durango address. The La Plata County Seat of Durango lay in the same direction as the ride home for Steve, but more than an hour beyond Lobos. That meant a two-hour drive, and he still had a lot of work to do. There was no way he could get there before seven. Steve hoped the seller would hold the rifle for them until they could get there. He quickly dialed the number.

The gentleman who answered couldn't have been more accommodating. When Steve explained his circumstances, the man politely interrupted. "Take your time," he said. "I'm holding it for you. Have dinner with your family and come over afterward with your son."

The rifle was just as Dalton imagined. The barrel was untarnished and the hardwood stock had the shine of fresh lacquer. The seller was even providing a vintage leather sheath, custom made for the weapon, and the gun manufacturer's original carton and instructions.

The gentleman explained that the vintage scope mounted atop the gun was a bit of a novelty. While modern devices were designed with round lenses, this scope featured a unique oval eyepiece, wider than it was tall. The unique shape translated directly to the user's perspective, providing increased peripheral vision, a useful benefit when tracking running animals, or God forbid, spotting a stalking predator on the flank. Most importantly, the scope provided magnification up to 20x, and featured a large light-enhancing diameter. At its maximum setting, images in the lens would appear one-twentieth their actual distance away, and the scope would perform extremely well in low light when game was most active.

The seller explained other intricacies of the hunting rifle. Like a parent leaving a child with a babysitter for the first time, he walked Dalton through a complete tear-down and re-assembly of the gun. Dalton watched closely as the man deliberately removed and re-attached the scope from the weapon. He took pictures with his phone and made mental notes. The rifle clearly meant a lot to the man, and he seemed pleased to see it go to somebody who would value it as he did.

On their drive back to Lobos, Dalton searched the brand and model of the distinctive scope on his phone. He found numerous positive reviews and noted a used unit for sale in the price range they'd paid for the gun and scope combined. "Dad," he said, "I think that guy gave us a heck of a good deal."

"You were lucky," Steve said, recognizing the tremendous value, "Mr. *Personals* Section."

Chapter 6

Gold Panners

D alton's new best friend, Jacob, had another interest and skill he was passing on, an activity that paid dividends, panning for gold in the local stream. Under Jacob's tutelage, Dalton had become quite adept at their new pastime.

The creek was running high from an overnight thunderstorm, and it was all Dalton could do to keep his footing; his quads and glutes were burning from trying to stay upright in the stream. He and Jacob had been panning hard for hours. For Dalton, it had been a particularly productive day. In addition to a good quantity of flakes, he'd found a small gold nugget.

Dalton figured out early-on, they weren't going to get rich panning. It was only logical; if there was a lot of gold and silver left around, the mines would still be operating. He roughly calculated the summer's payout-to-date was something slightly higher than minimum wage, even as the work was infinitely more strenuous than most jobs. Arduous as it was, panning on their own schedule was something they liked to do, especially on hot days with rewards like today's nugget.

It was well past noon and Dalton was hungry. "Let's take a break," he hollered to Jacob, his voice carrying over the roar of the rapids.

Jacob had been working equally hard in the frigid rain-swollen current, trying to match Dalton's haul. "Ten more minutes," he urged, staring down at his empty pan. He stepped to the middle of the stream, wading into the deep water to scrape gravel between a pair of submerged boulders. As he stepped toward the shallows to rinse the sand and rock from his pan, he realized Dalton was no longer in the creek. He looked to the bank where they'd set their spare clothing, but Dalton wasn't there. Jacob grew concerned; he lowered his tray, releasing its contents to the current. He picked a course to where they'd entered the water, passing below the worst of the rapids to where the water pooled and a slow eddy churned. As he waded below the torrent, a clamp came down on his calf like a slamming car door. "What the hell?" he hollered, breaking loose and crashing to the bank.

Dalton emerged from the water, giddy with laughter. "Alligator. Alligator!" he screamed.

Jacob stared at his friend in relieved disgust. "More like a toothless turtle," he said. "I thought you drowned."

"Thanks for caring," Dalton said.

Jacob peered at Dalton. "Well, payback's a bitch; remember that."

After a creek-side change into dry clothes, Dalton and Jacob headed toward Breitling's. The boys didn't spend much of their free time in town, but they did enjoy their trips to the grocery store. The local shop had a selection of salty snacks and sugary drinks they didn't usually find at home. A craving for quick calories was always a good excuse to consume junk food.

As they walked along, Dalton purposely jiggled his gold nugget in his pocket, rattling it among his change. "I love that sound," he taunted.

"Ten minutes more," Jacob argued, "that's all I needed."

"Maybe this afternoon, my friend," Dalton said. "But watch out for the gators."

They were still a few hundred yards outside of town when they saw Max Breitling exit the back of his shop. He awkwardly carried several unevenly stacked boxes to an older minivan. The vehicle was faded and showing signs of rust, a quality below the standard of his modern and well-stocked store.

The load Breitling carried seemed to warrant multiple trips. Somehow, he sat the boxes down without dumping them and triggered the locks with a remote key. He slid the cartons through the sliding side-panel opposite the driver's seat and climbed in, closing the door. As Dalton and Jacob approached the store, Breitling sped by. They waved, but the man failed to reciprocate.

Finding the store open was a relief. Mrs. Breitling seemed to have everything under control and was as friendly as ever. Dalton bought a French bread pizza and Jacob picked out a burrito. They nuked their purchases in the store's microwave and headed outside.

As they enjoyed their lunch on the sidewalk, Jacob gazed at the perpetually illuminated *Open* sign of the antique shop across the street. "Finish up," he urged. "Let's see if there's anything new at Taber's."

Dalton had never heard the antique store referred to as Taber's, nor had he been back since he and his dad stopped by and found it closed. He took the last bite of his pizza and placed the wrapper in a trash can.

The front door of the antique store was propped open by a blacksmith's anvil. Dalton was fairly sure it was authentic; the tool was beat-up and covered in soot. Aside from the sign advertising coins for sale, the door-prop looked more interesting than anything else in the store.

Dalton followed Jacob inside. The smell of the dank air reminded him of his grandparents' basement. The showroom looked unoccupied. "Hello, anybody here?" Dalton said, announcing their presence.

The dimly lit display area was configured from two rooms of a converted residence. The retrofit space looked like a do-it-yourself job. The removed wall had evidently been load-bearing; the ceiling sloped from both ends toward the middle where the barrier had been. The plaster work was rough, the paint colors of their respective walls mismatched. Jacob walked over to the store's coin case and scanned dates and mint designations in the selection. He doubted there was anything new since his last visit, but there was always a chance he'd missed something.

Dalton moved to Jacob's side, still looking for a store clerk. He cleared his throat to gather attention. "Hello," he said again.

A screech of chair legs across a wooden floor resonated above them. Clopping uneven footsteps moved across the sloped ceiling toward a stairwell behind the counter. A middle-aged man descended the steps and entered the room. "Yes?" Horrance Taber said, glaring alternately at Dalton and Jacob.

Taber was a slender middle-aged man with a thinning slicked-back mane, more grey than black. He was badly in need of a shave, his skin abnormally pale for the time of year. He lifted a cigarette for a drag revealing a disproportionately large forearm, his physique resembling the guy at the gym who uses only one machine.

Jacob straightened up from the cabinet, acknowledging the man. "Hello Mr. Taber," he said, nodding in the shopkeeper's direction. He was used to gruff treatment from the character. He wasn't surprised by Taber's tardy arrival or curt greeting.

Dalton followed Jacob's example, greeting Taber. "Hello Sir," he said. He couldn't take his eyes off the man's beastly forearms. He imagined naval tattoos beneath his short sleeves. "We're just having a look at your coins," he said. "Nice."

"What can I do for the two of you?" Taber said.

"I'm just showing Dalton around. He's new in town." Jacob knew the coins in Taber's shop were less than impressive, most contemporary and made of inexpensive alloys, worth little more than face value. The few older coins to be seen were severely worn, their dates barely legible.

Dalton hadn't actually gotten around to looking into the cabinet, and based on his misguided compliment, Taber probably knew it. Dalton again addressed the shopkeeper. "Do you have any gold coins?" he asked, "We've been panning outside town and—." Dalton fell silent. The sting of Jacob's hidden finger diving into his ribcage told him to shut up.

"—and we haven't had a bit of luck," Jacob said, picking up where Dalton left off. "Do you know of any good spots, Mr. Taber?"

"No," the shopkeeper replied simply.

"Thanks anyway, sir," Jacob said, politely. "Probably see you next weekend." He led Dalton over the anvil and out the door.

"Sorry about the prod back there, buddy," Jacob said. "I just never trust anyone with my sources."

"No worries," Dalton replied, "I guess you don't want that guy dipping into your honey-hole. You have enough competition already." He jingled the gold nugget in his pocket, smiling.

Taber watched from behind the counter as the visitors exited. He saw Jacob give his friend a playful shove. "Nothing better to do than play grab-ass and harass me," he said aloud. He inspected the coin cabinet latch. The lock was detached, but he had a habit of forgetting to secure it after transferring the coins from his safe each morning. He scanned his inventory, alternately glancing at Dalton and Jacob through the window. "*Panning for gold?*" he thought. "*Good luck with that.*"

Taber quickly wiped the finger smudges from the glass counter above his coins with a dirty rag and walked into his showroom. Through a side window of the converted house, he saw two cars parked outside the next structure down the valley. *"The new kid,"* he thought. He moved back past the coin cabinet and climbed the stairs. The coin case's lock sat uselessly on the counter.

Chapter 7

Stretching the Rules

Dalton and Jacob were hot and bored, sitting on Dalton's front steps at midday. "Let's hike up the mountain across the valley and test the cool air flowing from that boarded-up mine," Jacob said, appearing to ignore his normal sensibilities.

"Are you nuts?" Dalton protested. "If the mine doesn't kill us, our parents will."

Jacob recognized his suggestion lacked proper nuance. "Not in the mine, near the mine," he said. "We can sit by the opening where the boards have fallen away. Cold air's pouring out. I've done it before."

Jumping over chain link fences and ducking clotheslines, Dalton and Jacob beelined over the neighboring yards of the narrow valley toward the adjacent mountain. As they crossed the town's three crushed-rock roads, dust clouds rose in the dry air. Dalton trailed Jacob by several steps as they cut across the last property before their ascent. He managed to stay ahead of a pursuing spaniel as its owner dropped her laundry basket and chased after the dog. The woman managed to gather the animal just as the boys reached the primitive trailhead.

The path's ascent was more climb than hike, suited better to goats than young men. Scrub trees rooted in rock and shallow soil provided useful handholds as Dalton and Jacob pulled themselves upward, their feet slipping on the stony mountain face. Where there was nothing to take hold of, they placed their hands directly on the rock, walking simultaneously with their arms and legs for balance. The trail finally merged with a less severe path, cutting directly to the camp. The gradient was tamer, allowing Dalton and Jacob to pick up their pace.

They emerged on the downhill side of the camp, on the opposite lateral side of the mineshaft. The landscape was barren. The mine's tailings, broken extracted rock, lay several feet deep, inhibiting vegetative growth. Dalton and Jacob worked their way between the dilapidated buildings toward the boarded-up mineshaft. Wisps of cool air from the deep earth brushed their sweat-soaked skin as they approached the tunnel. At the rim of the pit, they met the full force of the chilly air. It was spiked with the smell of mold and rotting wood.

The shaft entrance had long been boarded up, though many planks had fallen away. Dalton wanted a closer look and called out to Jacob, "Let me see your phone light. Mine's broke," he said.

Jacob passed it over.

As Dalton peered into the shaft, he was confused by the mine's configuration. "This thing goes straight down," he said. "How'd they get the rock out?"

"Actually, they didn't take much out here," Jacob replied. "Only what was needed to open it. This is a vent shaft. It's just for air. The silver came out other places." He pointed at another well-hidden shaft opening within eyeshot. A rockslide had buried most of it. "That was the main shaft, I suppose," Jacob continued. "It's called an adit. They're bigger. They may have had a rail-system up here at one time. The miners would dig back the adit until they found silver, then they'd follow the vein."

"So, the tunnel starts in straight and then just goes in any direction, helter-skelter?" Dalton asked.

"Actually, the adits go, more or less, straight back," Jacob explained. "When the miners would hit a vein of silver, they'd follow it with a side-tunnel, a drift. Drifts can go in any direction."

Dalton couldn't help being tempted by a short excursion down the mine. The subterranean design Jacob described sounded fascinating and the heat outside was oppressive. The young men extended their legs as deeply as they could into the vent shaft as they drank from their water bottles. When Dalton had cooled off some, he stood and started walking in the direction of the camp. "Let's see what's in those old buildings," he shouted over his shoulder.

In addition to the waterwheel, there were three buildings in the camp. Two were largely disintegrated, only partial walls remained. One retained its integrity.

Dalton and Jacob circled the intact building. The entire structure leaned starkly downhill. They found the door open, wedged ajar by the building's settling.

The shack consisted of a single cluttered room, surprisingly well-lit, courtesy of direct sunlight through a broken window. Dust clouds boiled in the sun's rays as Dalton and Jacob sorted through the debris scattered across the shattered floorboards. An old stove lay askew in the corner of the barracks. Some unidentifiable iron tools were visible among the rubble, all corroded beyond scrap. Straightening up to stretch his back, Dalton noticed some graffiti on the wall. The nature of the vulgar message suggested it hadn't been there long. "I guess we're not the only recent visitors," he said. "I can't imagine a local doing that."

Jacob looked at the foul message. "Nice," he responded.

Dalton stepped over piles of debris toward the vandalized wall, eyeing several additional irregularities on the vertical boards. Immediately to the right of the graffiti were four odd looking spots. The pale marks cut a contrast to the dark and moldy wood. Up close, it was clear the spots were holes, the incorrupt, inner layers of the timbers.

As Dalton probed a void with his finger, Jacob looked on. "It looks like somebody took a hammer to it," Jacob said.

Dalton pondered the scene a moment more. "I think they're bullet holes," he said. He drove his pocketknife deep into the recess, drilling and prying until an intact bullet popped out. "Told you," he said. "And it's no plinking bullet either. I'd say it's forty-caliber."

Jacob was intrigued. "That would have come from a pistol," he said. "There's nobody hunting up here with a gun like that."

Dalton adjusted his position to square up with a second hole, kicking away rubble to gain his footing. He drilled an identical bullet out of the wall and tossed it to Jacob. "A souvenir for each of us," he said, dropping the first slug in his pocket.

The loose rock below the mining camp made the trip down the mountain slower than the hike up. Dalton and Jacob concentrated on their footing, moving as quickly as possible, trying to keep their balance. At the bottom of the debris field, they entered a timber via a narrow trail. They were startled by a horse whinny, just feet away.

"Morning boys," a mounted equestrian said. "See anything interesting up there?" Recently elected Sheriff Thero Buford sat atop his horse. His posture projected his new position and authority.

Jacob knew the man and spoke up. "Morning Sheriff", he said. "We were just cooling off up there by the vent-shaft of the old mine. Have you met Dalton Wallace? He's new in town."

"Nice to meet you Dalton," the sheriff said. "I heard your family moved into the old Tucker place." Buford turned his attention back to Jacob. "Son, you know better than to be messing around near these mines. You set a bad example for your friend, here. Every year seems like we pull a dead flatlander out of one of these holes, treasure hunters, most of 'em."

Immediately, an unevenly folded wad of paper fell out of the sheriff's pocket and tumbled to the ground. "Give that to me," he barked at Jacob, snatching the package from him as quickly as he could reach it from his horse.

Buford paused, gathering his thoughts. "You know," he said, "I heard Ben Childress had been messing around this mine before his father supposedly swept him off to California. Did you and Ben ever come up here, Jacob?"

"No Sir," Jacob answered. He could see where the sheriff was going with his question. "Do you think Ben might have gotten lost in the mine?"

"I don't want anybody getting worried, unnecessarily," Buford said. "Let's just hope we get some good news from California soon."

The sheriff removed his hat and wiped his brow with a handkerchief. He pulled the left rein of his tack, turning the horse back up the trail. "Anyway, you boys say hello to your folks," he said. He spat tobacco juice at the horse's feet and moved uphill toward the mine.

B uford tied up his horse in the shade of the dilapidated waterwheel of the Winning Stakes Mine. A moderate flow of spring and glacial waters ran beneath its shattered paddles. The gelding bent down to drink.

The sheriff struck out on foot, bypassing the camp's barracks and partially-exposed vent shaft. He proceeded uphill to the remnants of a major rockslide. A depression in the broken stone exposed traces of wooden debris. Buford squatted, sorting the small pieces of timber from the rock, trying to differentiate fallen trees from milled lumber. He stepped into the dip, kicking at larger rocks, jumping up and down, trying to detect movement in the rubble.

A bright reflection between Buford's leather boots brought him to his knees. Beneath a shallow layer of pine needles and sand, a round, flat metal object projected silvery rays. The sheriff's heart raced and his respiration became heavy as he brushed away the debris and soil.

Buford breathed a heavy sigh as he plucked the item from the ground, a newish tin lid. "Filthy tourists," he said.

Working his way downhill below the camp and rubble, Buford diverged from the stream. A second boarded-up mineshaft was visible in a small grove of young firs. He walked over, observing the shaft's entrance, sealed tight. He circled around the grove, looking for the mine's vent shaft or another opening to the underground complex.

Buford hiked lower on the mountain in the direction of the creek. Additional groves of young fir and spruce sprouted from the stone. He wove his way through the wooden and rock tapestry looking for signs of the mine and trying to keep his bearings. Finding no further borings, he turned uphill to return to the camp. The top of the waterwheel was visible over the green canopy. He cut a straight line, bushwhacking back toward his horse.

As Buford approached the camp, he realized he was on the opposite side of the stream from his steed, although he couldn't remember crossing the watercourse. He gazed down the trifling creek as it twisted between the groves and stone. *"It's so small, I probably stepped over it,"* he thought. Buford pulled the wad of papers from his pocket and made several notes.

Chapter 8

A Familiar Face

For Dalton, the transition from summer vacation to a new school year was always difficult, but scaling back his new hobbies and entering a new school made this year especially tough. The sophomore class Dalton was joining had already spent a year together, some of the students longer in middle school and earlier. Dalton would be attending Jefferson High in Montrose. While Lobos lay in Ouray County, certain geographical areas had been swapped with Montrose County for logistical reasons. Driving around any given mountain, or bridging a river, could add dozens of miles to a trip in the San Juan Mountains, inflating transportation costs for local governments and inconveniencing families. In Dalton's case, attending Jefferson High cut his commute miles in half.

Jacob Burrell also attended Jefferson. Although he was just a month older than Dalton, he was a year ahead in school. Jacob helped Dalton with his on-line scheduling, and the friends were able to arrange a history class and their lunch periods together. Dalton and Jacob would be joined at school by two other Lobos youths, Ben Childress, when or if he returned from California, and Jimmy Irwin. Jacob had introduced Dalton to Jimmy early-on that summer, but Jimmy hadn't been around much. He'd spent most of his break in Europe doing a study abroad program.

The Tuesday following Labor Day was the first day of school in southwest Colorado. Even though it was still summer, the morning air was crisp, bordering on cold. Weather forecasters were already showing the possibility of snow in the higher elevations in their extended forecasts. As Dalton strode toward the bus stop, he observed frosty patches of grass in the low-laying yards of town. The dry air carried a pleasant metallic fragrance like something he'd experienced in Kansas, though much later in the year. A westerly breeze caught him from behind, penetrating his loose-fitting sweatshirt. The wind provoked a shiver.

The bus stop was on Main Street, in front of Breitling's Store. On that first morning of school, it was no surprise to Dalton that Jacob and Jimmy were the only other students waiting. Dalton hadn't seen Jimmy since he returned from London. "Hey big guy," he said, "It's been a while."

"What's up, Dalton?" Jimmy said in a deep monotone voice. Jimmy was a year older than Jacob, starting his senior year. He was literally the big-man on campus, standing six-feet, four inches tall. His orange freckles and red hair stood-out in a crowd. Jimmy was a three-sport athlete, excelling in football. But his physical prowess was exceeded by his smarts and ambition. In eleven months, he'd be heading to the Ivy League as a student-athlete. He had his choice of schools. In addition to book-smarts, Jimmy was quick-witted, though his natural competitiveness and intelligence sometimes came across as arrogant.

Right on schedule, the school bus arrived, and the Lobos trio filed in. Aside from the driver, the bus was empty. As the three Lobos youths descended the bus aisle, Jacob and Jimmy spoke busily about a friend they hadn't seen since school let out, somebody Dalton didn't know. Dalton's friends slid into a seat halfway back. Dalton took the bench across from them.

The ride to Montrose was anything but direct, traversing one gravel road after another. Dust clouds from passing motorists hung in narrow valleys, their fine white particles coating the leaves of nearby trees. The bus's engine strained in low gears as it labored up exhaustive hills. The corresponding descents on the machine's stiff suspension and relatively narrow wheelbase were like bobsled runs without banked turns. The transmission whirred and the exhaust pipe belched out black smoke as the driver downshifted to control his speed.

There were stations along the way that in Dalton's mind made Lobos look big, many stops for single students. Private roads and driveways intersected the route, some maintained better than the county roads, others muddy or overgrown by weeds. The number of mailboxes at any given stop sent a signal about the number of students that would board, though on a couple of occasions there was no sign of a driveway or postal marker at all. The kids appeared to emerge from the forest like ghosts.

After twenty minutes, the bus finally made its way back onto blacktop. Dalton was completely spun around and not at all sure where they were. The sign for Querido was unexpected. The route Dalton's family took for pizza, or to visit other restaurants, was far more direct. More than a dozen students waited for the bus in front of the town's lone gas station.

In the weeks preceding the start of the school year, Dalton thought often about the possibility of seeing Cheyanne outside of her family's restaurant. But running into her on the bus was not something he'd considered. The sudden realization that he could be face-to-face with the beautiful waitress at any moment made him nervous.

On board the bus, kids had been trying to hold onto double seats, but the large haul at the Querido stop meant everyone would have to share. Students began moving and shifting, each trying to land near his or her better friend. Even though Jacob and Jimmy were near, all the jockeying made Dalton uncomfortable. He nonchalantly slid closer to the aisle and his friends, placing his backpack strategically in the window seat. Not that anyone had shown any interest in sitting with him.

Bundled-up Querido teens piled into the bus and paraded the aisle, a few dropping out near the front. Dalton struggled to see the faces of the new arrivals across the crowded bus rows and shifting procession. The last rider crested the bus steps and took a seat in the first row as the remaining passengers looked for seats. Dalton didn't see her. Apparently, Cheyanne had other transportation to school.

A hooded figure suddenly stopped uncomfortably close to Dalton in the aisle. "Can I sit there?" Cheyanne asked, raising her eyes to the empty window-seat next to Dalton.

"Sure," Dalton said. He moved his backpack to the floor and slid over to the window, leaving the aisle seat empty for Cheyanne. He'd recognized her voice even before he saw her familiar green eyes and soft features.

Cheyanne removed her backpack and slid her petite frame into the aisle seat next to Dalton. She pealed back her hoodie and collected her long auburn hair from the back of her sweatshirt, swinging it over one shoulder towards the aisle. "I'm Cheyanne," she said, smiling.

It had been a couple of weeks since Dalton last saw Cheyanne at her family's restaurant. He hadn't been lucky enough to get her as his server in over a month. He'd never seen her made-up. A touch of eye shadow and blush accentuated her stunning features. Faint, alternating wafts of Cheyanne's floral shampoo and candied lip gloss pervaded the intimate space between them. "I know who you are," Dalton said, "You introduce yourself every time you serve our table at your restaurant." Conversing with attractive members of the opposite sex had always challenged Dalton's poise. He nervously forgot to introduce himself.

"What's your name?" Cheyanne asked. "You're new around here, aren't you?"

"Dalton," he replied plainly. He awkwardly presented his hand for a shake.

"I've seen you at the restaurant a few times," Cheyanne said, accepting Dalton's hand.

Dalton was pleased to have been noticed. His nerves lessened. "Yeah, we moved here from Kansas," he said. "I live in Lobos, but we eat at your family's restaurant all the time. We love it."

"Thanks," Cheyanne said, moving her gaze to the back of the bench in front of them.

Dalton was afraid that was the end of it, just some small talk in appreciation for the seat. He was too anxious to initiate further and turned toward the window.

"So, are you a junior or a senior?" Cheyanne said, finally.

"Sophomore," he replied.

"Me too," she said.

Dalton was just becoming comfortable when a jealous Jimmy Irwin chimed in, "Cheyanne," he said, "be careful around Dalton. He's prone to motion sickness."

Dalton grinned knowingly across the aisle at the older student.

Cheyanne glared at Jimmy in subtle contempt. She was used to competition for her attention, and she recognized what the upperclassman was up to. "Europe was good for you, Jimmy. Very sophisticated," she said. She turned her back toward the aisle to learn more about the new Coloradan.

Chapter 9

The Mines

A hand-made map laid on the desk in front of Sheriff Buford, an amalgamation of legal-size paper sheets, painstakingly taped together. Ink-lines crisscrossed the canvas, muting where the pen bridged the tape-joints. Crease marks from inconsistent foldings zigzagged the map's sketches and notes. A stain from horse manure blotted a corner, a remnant from when it was dropped the day before.

The sheriff took a sip of coffee from a foam cup. The plastic tab on the safety-lid opened unexpectedly wide, sending a scalding rush of hot liquid over his tongue. "Blasted," he cried. He pealed the cap off the cup and threw it in the direction of a trash can, missing. He folded the map and placed it in his shirt pocket.

Despite the constant underground temperature of fifty-five degrees in the mine, Buford was burning up in the high humidity. He was a heavy man, and it didn't take much for him to work up a lather. Buford navigated to the spot he'd left off the last time he was in the mine. An old collapse partially blocked his way and there was a lot of work to be done. The debris would have to be cleared before he could proceed.

Buford labored in the tunnel, clearing stone after stone, until the gap was wide enough for his girth. He leveraged himself through the excavated space and descended deeper into the mountain. Playing the beam of his flashlight out front, he followed the drift mine through its twists and turns. He had entered new territory, beyond the scope of his experience and map. A sharp turn lay directly ahead. Buford's anticipation of a breakthrough sored.

"Dead friggen end," he screamed, as his flashlight illuminated the tunnel's termination point. He drew back his arm, ready to pitch his light into the rock wall. He slumped to the floor, taking a knee. *"All right then—,"* he thought, gathering himself, *"—from the start."* He pulled a canteen from his belt for a drink, opened his map, and positioned his flashlight over its center.

T he weekend was near, and Dalton and Jacob had their free-time mapped out. On Saturday, they planned to shop for items needed for their upcoming deer hunt. Jacob's dad had other business in Grand Junction and agreed to help Dalton and Jacob sell their panned gold, before dropping them off at the sporting goods super store to spend the proceeds. Aside from church on Sunday, the rest of the weekend would be spent setting deer blinds and sighting-in their rifle scopes.

When Dalton got home from school on Friday, he was surprised to see both of his parents at home. The mood in the house was decidedly muted. Dalton's widowed grandmother, Susan's mom, was hospitalized in Omaha and was undergoing tests. A fainting spell had resulted in a good-sized bump on the head. She'd been alone at the time and things could have gone worse. She was doing fine but needed further evaluation. Although two of Dalton's aunts lived close by, his mom wanted to be there.

Steve and Susan didn't want Dalton to miss school so early in the school year, and there was a good chance they wouldn't be back before Monday. There was also Dalton and Jacob's planned trip to Grand Junction with Mr. Burrell. A quick phone call determined it would be okay for Dalton to stay with Jacob's family.

Dalton's parents drove out of Lobos early Saturday morning. After the boys saw them off at their home, they had a few free minutes before leaving for Grand Junction. Steve Wallace had volunteered a pruning saw to help the boys build their blinds for deer season and told Dalton he would find it in the basement. Dalton asked Jacob to help him look for it.

The boys searched the dusty shelves, opening numerous boxes and totes, but the saw was nowhere to be found. An alarm from Jacob's phone chirped. It was time to meet his father for their trip. They ascended the abrupt stairs from the cellar, Jacob first and Dalton close behind. But Dalton stopped halfway, his eye drawn through the stair slats to the foundation wall behind. He spun round and leapt back to the basement floor.

"Where are you going?" Jacob said, sensing he'd lost his trailer.

"I see something," replied Dalton.

"The saw?"

"No, something else," Dalton said, "Come down."

Jacob found Dalton behind the staircase examining the basement wall, tracing his hand along the plaster-coated stone. From Jacob's perspective, it looked like every other cellar wall in Lobos. "What are you doing?" he asked anxiously. "My dad's probably out there. We gotta go!"

Dalton appeared impervious to his friend's urgings. He ran his hand along the wall vertically above his head, and then across at a right angle. "I think it's a door," he said.

Jacob circled around the staircase for a closer look. "A what?"

"It's a hidden door, or something," Dalton said, as Jacob arrived at his side. "Look how the plaster protrudes, and these tiny cracks shaped like a rectangle."

Jacob nodded. He could finally see the shape.

Dalton grabbed a metal putty knife from a nearby shelf, pondering the implications of knocking down the plaster. "My parents will kill me if I tear this place up," he said. "I'll just knock out a small spot that's ready to go." He struck the wall with the handle of the putty knife. A quarter-size piece of plaster fell to the ground, exposing dark and aged wood. "This house backs into the mountain like the rest of the buildings on this side of the street," he said. "This wall should be solid rock, like the rest of the foundation."

"Maybe they framed it up to look nice," Jacob suggested.

"True, but why would they put a door in it?" Dalton said. "This shape has the orientation and size of a man-door. Anyway, the other three walls of the foundation are exposed stone."

"There's only one way to find out," Jacob said.

Dalton began prying away plaster with the business end of the putty knife. The plaster broke easily and fell to the ground. He worked his way down the left side of the rectangle towards the floor. "You work the other side," he instructed, handing Jacob a Swiss Army toolset he carried in his pocket.

The two had the outline exposed in less than a minute. They stood silently, staring at a perfectly formed wooden rectangle. Dalton pounded his fist lightly in the center of the frame. "Hear that?" he said.

"Hear what?" Jacob replied, incredulously.

"It sounds hollow," Dalton said, pounding harder.

Jacob's cellphone rang-out a familiar ring. It was his father. Dalton and Jacob exchanged a confused and fascinated glance. "We need to go," Jacob said, finally.

"We'll figure this out later," Dalton said. "If it's anything, my parents need to know about it. If not, we need to patch this wall up."

The anomaly in the basement wasn't discussed on the way to Grand Junction. Dalton left it to his friend's judgment, and Jacob never brought it up. They passed three *We Buy Gold* signs in Grand Junction before arriving at a traditional jewelry store. The shop was owned by a friend of Mr. Burrell. He and his wife had bought their wedding rings there.

"This is it boys," Mr. Burrell said. "Time to cash-in on all that panning."

As luck would have it, gold was trading at a decade's high. Dalton and Jacob each walked away with more than $700 in cash. The next stop was the sporting-goods store. Jacob's dad dropped them off in the parking lot and left for his appointment.

The store was one of the boy's favorite places. In addition to a seemingly limitless selection of outdoor supplies, the big-box's unique decorations and atmosphere were simply over-the-top. Dalton and Jacob were met at the entrance by a four-story atrium rimmed by a facade of mountain ridges that looked nearly as real as the ones surrounding Lobos. Graduating levels of wilderness scenes supported mounted elk, mule-deer, bears, coyotes, and other small game, taxidermy artistically on par with the mountain setting they adorned. A massive grizzly bear with a trout locked in its jaws stood next to a swimming pool-sized aquarium filled with native Colorado fishes. A massive bull-moose raised his head from the water, his antler spread wider than either Dalton or Jacob was tall. There were so many magnificent mounts, it was almost like visiting a museum.

Dalton and Jacob were inspecting and trying on hunting boots; Dalton needed a warm pair and Jacob's money was simply burning a hole in his pocket.

Dalton had narrowed his choice down to two models but needed a bathroom break. He left Jacob in the shoe department and hustled to the back of the store.

Jacob sensed where Dalton was going with his boot choice and pulled the box with his size from the shelf. He took the boots from the box and positioned them carefully in-line with the numerous display models on a show board, separating left and right to hide his handywork. He grabbed the empty box and quickly proceeded to the store's atrium and abundance of lifelike mounted animals.

The Massasauga Rattle Snake he chose was common to Grand Junction and the lower regions of the Rockies. It was also among the finest likenesses in the store. Its form lay appropriately coiled in a width comparable to the shoebox, its head surging forward with mouth open, mid-strike. Jacob looked over both shoulders and delicately loaded the mount into the box, covering the wooden mounting stand with the shoes' tissue paper. He hustled back to the shoe department and placed the carton where he'd found it, between the smaller and larger sizes of the same brand and design.

Dalton appeared sporting a new camouflage stocking cap. "I'm going to be warm on top and bottom," he said.

"Nice," Jacob said. "Which boots did you decide on?"

"I'm going with the Danners," Dalton replied. "Made in the USA."

Jacob inwardly sighed in relief. His hunch had been correct. "You better try them on one more time," he said, "it's a big investment."

Dalton sorted out the last pair of size tens from the rack. He peeled off both his tennis shoes and moved the box to his lap. As he lifted the lid, he let out a howl like a twelve-year old girl and tossed the box in the air. He jumped on top of the fitting bench in his socks, hopping up and down like the seat was on fire.

Jacob dove toward the floor, snatching the expensive animal mount from the air like the *immaculate reception*. He jumped to his feet, carefully placing the mounted snake on a display table.

Dalton sneered at his mischievous friend.

Jacob tossed Dalton his new boots from the display shelf. "Remember what I said back at the creek?" he said. "About how payback's a bitch? Try the boots on while I take this snake back to its pit."

Flush with necessary hunting supplies and various frivolities, Dalton and Jacob arrived back in Lobos with plenty of afternoon sunshine remaining. They took advantage of the daylight and comfortable temperature, checking for fresh signs of deer and setting up a pair of makeshift blinds with fallen trees and branches. As they hiked back into town, Dalton got a text from his mom.

GRANDMA'S FINE. COMING HOME TOMORROW, LATE

The next morning after church, Dalton and Jacob hiked out to the Halstead Ranch with their hunting mentor, Jacob's dad. Mr. Burrell's experience and expertise made sighting-in their rifles a cinch. The prowess Dalton had shown with a twenty-two translated well to his more powerful gun. The elder Burrell saw for himself what Jacob had previously described; Dalton was an excellent marksman.

Despite their optimistic estimates, Mr. and Mrs. Wallace didn't arrive in Lobos until nearly eight Sunday night. Mrs. Burrell recognized their predicament and had dinner waiting for them. The families shared the meal and the Wallace's returned home late.

It wasn't until he climbed into bed that Dalton's mind returned to the peculiar wooden form he and Jacob revealed on the wall of the cellar. He resolved to sort the issue out the following day.

Chapter 10

Land of the Missing

The long bumpy bus ride to Querido seemed especially long to Dalton Monday morning. As exhilarating as the prospect of the busy weekend had been, the thought of five uninterrupted school days seemed more impactful. Only the anticipation of seeing Cheyanne seemed to cheer him up.

The bus finally pulled into Querido, but Cheyanne didn't board. Dalton's cloudy day was looking like rain. He considered asking one of the local kids where she was, but he didn't want to appear to be too interested. He wished he could text her, but he hadn't gained the courage to ask her for her number. He resigned himself to see if she'd made it in by other means or catch up with her the following day.

Jacob was seated on the bus across the aisle from Dalton. He was speaking with Jimmy Irwin, seated on the window next to him. Jimmy was carrying the conversation in an oddly somber tone. One by one, students in front and behind their seat began to lean over and listen. Jacob stretched across the aisle and addressed Dalton, "You need to hear this."

"Jimmy, start over," Dalton said, calling out to his older friend.

"Sure," Jimmy said. "You know Ben Childress, right?"

Dalton nodded affirmatively, though he hadn't actually had the chance to meet the kid.

"Well," Jimmy continued, "it turns out his dad out in California doesn't know where Ben is. His mom is super upset about it. She's staying with her parents in Montrose. They live on the same street as my grandparents."

An older student Dalton didn't know spoke up, "He's a goner," he said, "but that's nothing new around here. Ben makes four."

Jacob chimed in, "My parents told me about the other three, but that was down in La Plata county, a long time ago, before we were even born. The guy got caught and was sent to prison."

All of which was true.

O ver the course of two years, starting in the early two-thousands, three teenage boys had gone missing in nearby La Plata County. Two of the young men had never been found. The third, a boy named Joshua Vernon, was found dead.

On the night of Joshua's disappearance, Thero Buford had been a rookie deputy with the La Plata County Sheriff's Department. Ironically, Buford had been the only on-shift officer not assigned to the search; he was left on his regular beat. He reasoned that somebody had to be in charge in the county seat of Durango; he'd been given a special responsibility. The truth was the local sheriff knew Buford lacked experience.

Coincidentally, there had been another incident in the normally quiet San Juan Mountain region that day. Before Buford's shift, an extremely bold shoplifter stuffed his shirt at a convenience mart and dashed out in broad daylight. The store clerk reported the suspect was a white male in his early twenties, medium height, wearing a grey stocking cap. He fled north in a white, early model Toyota. A bulletin had been placed with state law-enforcement agencies, but the car hadn't been spotted. Buford kept his eyes peeled and stayed close to his radio as he made his regular rounds, keeping advised of both searches.

In the early morning following his shift, Deputy Buford drove his cruiser toward his home in nearby Bayfield. Although exhausted, returning to his humble residence was not something he looked forward to. The mobile home had a residual odor from its previous owner, a sickening smell that had been hidden with deodorizers when the trailer was on the market. Buford had been meaning to buy a fresh bottle.

As the deputy pulled into Bayfield, he saw the lights of large houses and vacation homes in the hills above town. "Texans," he said to himself, "all hat and no cattle." Buford resented transplants, especially wealthy ones. He considered stopping for a cup of coffee but realized it would disrupt his nocturnal schedule. He decided to get a breakfast sandwich and headed downtown where he'd have his pick of fast-food drive-throughs. He picked up a value meal and turned toward home. As Buford devoured his sandwich, he pondered the day's events. *"Maybe the thief doubled back through Durango and headed in a different direction,"* he thought. *"Maybe east, over this way."*

As the deputy drove down the town's main drive, he inspected the parking lots of the town's two motels, situated side by side. Seeing no car matching the given description, he drove around the block to go home. As he made the final turn, he glimpsed a car in his rearview mirror parked behind the motels' shared garbage corral. Circling back, he found a small white Toyota, crammed tightly between the buildings and the dumpsters.

As Buford steered into the motel lot through the rear drive, a dark figure darted between buildings and disappeared into a stairwell. The deputy parked his cruiser, dimmed his lights, and turned off the ignition. He exited the vehicle, and quietly closed the door. Buford drew his service revolver, retreating to the back of the complex. He circled the building and stealthily approached the breezeway, hugging the wall to keep his body and shadow concealed. Buford's strategy paid off. His approach brought him directly behind the hidden suspect. The only exit for the perpetrator was through the deputy and his loaded gun.

With the suspect cuffed and locked in the back of his cruiser, the young deputy called in his status and location. Buford walked back to the stairway to look for evidence while he waited for back-up. A large object underneath the bottom step of the stairwell caught his eye. He put on his gloves and cautiously reached below. It was an article of clothing, a hooded sweatshirt. Buford carried the hoody out into the low light of a streetlamp. The dark fabric was damp. He moved his hand close to his face. His gloved fingers were wet with an oily red substance, blood. The deputy sprinted back to his squad car, grabbing his radio handset. "Where is my back-up?" he shouted. "We have an assault, and possible homicide. Victim unidentified."

Buford didn't wait for a response from dispatch. He threw the mic on the seat, re-drew his weapon, and walked toward the suspect's car. Circling the white sedan, Buford shined his powerful tactical flashlight on the car's seats and floorboards. There was no sign of a victim or struggle. At the rear of the car, he noticed a strip of denim fabric protruding from the closed trunk. He tried to lift the hood, but it was latched and locked. He ran to his cruiser and opened the trunk. He quickly located a heavy iron crowbar and returned to the Toyota. In seconds, the deputy pried open the latch. Buford's suspicions were confirmed; the bloodied body of Joshua Vernon lay inside.

The bus screeched to a stop in front of Jefferson High and Dalton hustled out ahead of Jacob and Jimmy. He made an excuse about needing to see a teacher before class, but all of them knew where he was going.

Cheyanne's locker was closed and locked. There was no sign of her.

Rumors about Ben Childress' disposition were not reserved to Jimmy Irwin or the students from the bus. Everyone at school seemed to have an opinion about Ben's whereabouts and fate. The situation became so distracting, the school's assistant-principle addressed the student-body via intercom during third period, the class Dalton shared with Jacob. The administrator stressed there was no reason to believe anything bad had happened to the teen. When the announcement was finished, most of the teachers picked up on the subject with their respective classrooms. Dalton and Jacob's teacher pointed out that California was a long way away, and that Ben Childress' domestic situation was anything but clear. Dalton appreciated that the faculty was trying to keep everybody calm, but there was no denying the whole situation was scary.

Jacob leaned across the aisle in their classroom and spoke discreetly to Dalton, "It seems to me, they need to get Ben's parents in the same room and get this thing sorted out," he said.

Dalton pondered Jacob's suggestion, not knowing Ben or his parents. "True," he said, "but in the meantime, somebody might want to organize a prayer at the flagpole."

Jacob nodded in agreement.

The bell rang and Dalton and Jacob headed for the classroom door. Dalton felt his phone vibrate in his pocket. He pulled the device out to check the message, but he didn't recognize the number.

IT'S ME, CHEYANNE. MEET ME OUT THE SIDE GATE IN THE NEIGHBORHOOD. WE'RE GOING TO LUNCH

Dalton was shocked, wondering where she got his number. A second text followed.

BRING JACOB IF YOU WANT

"That's who," Dalton thought. He held up his phone for Jacob to read. "What about this?" he said.

"Well, she asked for it," Jacob said. "Let's go."

Their lunch hour was only fifty minutes long, barely enough time for fast food. Dalton and Jacob moved swiftly through the gym and mechanical shop, avoiding teachers and other staff. At the door, they quickly checked their surroundings and sprinted across a narrow drive to a sidewalk and stairs to an adjoining neighborhood. Cheyanne was parked outside the gate behind the wheel of her family's SUV. Dalton and Jacob swiftly climbed in, Dalton in the passenger seat, Jacob in the rear.

"What are you doing?" Dalton said to Cheyanne, smiling widely.

"I had a dentist appointment, first thing this morning," Cheyanne said. "I'm done, but who would know? Anyway, it's break time."

"I didn't even know you drove," Dalton said.

"Well, you missed my birthday," Cheyanne replied.

Dalton scanned his memory. He was sure it hadn't come up.

"Where are we going?" Jacob asked, buckling himself in on the rear bench.

"I don't care," Cheyanne said, "Anywhere but pizza."

They drove through at a burger joint and ate in the parking lot. As they sat in the shade sipping on the last of their soft drinks, Dalton thought of all the drama Cheyanne had missed that morning. "Hey, did you hear about Ben Childress?" he said.

Cheyanne sat up straight in her seat. "No, what about him?" she said.

"Jimmy said he's got inside information. Ben's not with his father in California. The whole school's buzzing."

"Let me guess," Cheyanne said, "it's about the missing kids down in Durango, from twenty years ago."

"Exactly," Dalton replied. He was surprised Cheyanne knew about the old situation, too.

Jacob spoke up, frustrated, "Well, Ben's my friend and this whole thing sucks."

"I hear you Jacob," Dalton said.

Cheyanne nodded sympathetically. She put the car in drive and steered them back to school. She dropped the guys off in the neighborhood and circled round to the parking lot, worrying about Ben. She brushed her teeth with her finger and popped in a breath mint before presenting herself at the school office to check in.

For Dalton, all the excitement made the day speed by. When the Lobos youths stepped off the bus that afternoon, Jimmy headed straight home to do homework. Dalton and Jacob walked toward the Wallace residence. Dalton's parents were still at work.

"Did you talk to your folks about that thing in your basement yet?" Jacob asked.

"No, I haven't had a chance," Dalton replied.

"Let's go figure it out," Jacob offered. "If it's nothing we'll patch the hole up. I've got some spackle at my house."

Within minutes, Dalton and Jacob were in the cellar. The image of the distinct form revealed by their previous excavation seemed to confirm, more than ever, it was a door of some kind. Dalton grabbed the putty knife and started chipping away at the plaster surrounded by the exposed wooden rectangle. Jacob worked alongside his friend with a chisel from Dalton's Swiss Army tool set. Two hinges and an adjacent low-profile latch were quickly exposed.

When he was sure the door was free, Dalton lifted the rusty latch, tugging it firmly with what grip he could muster. It didn't budge.

Jacob stepped in and gave it his best shot. Not so much as a wiggle.

Dalton spotted his dad's toolbox across the room. He sorted through the gear inside, trying to come up with an idea to pry the door open. "Here's a long screwdriver," he said finally. "It might do it."

The tool had a sturdy shank and oversized grip. Dalton placed the business end through a padlock hole in the latch. It fit perfectly. He put his foot on the wall outside of the door frame for leverage. Placing one hand on the screwdriver handle, and the other on the stem, he pulled with all his might. The door bowed to his force but quickly sprung back. He pulled again, mustering more force than his first attempt. The door gave, opening more than an inch. Cool musty air seeped from the void, pervading the cellar.

"Let me try," Jacob said, switching in.

The rusted hinges loosened, and the door opened sufficiently to allow Dalton to slip in sideways. "Come on," he urged Jacob.

"It's pitch-black in there," Jacob said, hesitating. "Is there a light switch or something?"

"Light switch?" Dalton said. "I don't think so, this is a mineshaft."

Chapter 11

Peculiar Anomaly

Dalton poked his head back into the cellar from the mine and directed Jacob to two flashlights. Jacob clicked on the lamps and squeezed through the door. They directed their beams down the adit shaft as they carefully moved in. Wooden supports lined the walls and ceiling of the tunnel, an organized pattern of sets every ten feet or so. The rock ceiling was barely sufficient for them to stand.

Just beyond the fifth set of supports, a divergent shaft exited to the right, a drift-shaft with a smaller diameter than the main tunnel. Dalton and Jacob played their lights into the void. The shaft moved in several feet before turning slightly right and downward. The texture and finish of the drift's walls appeared rougher and less refined than the main adit.

Dalton sensed danger. "We can't risk wandering into one of these," he said. "We need a rope or something to guide us down the main shaft, lead us back if we get lost or lose these lights."

"You're right," Jacob replied, recognizing the danger. "I saw a rope back in your basement. Let's go back and tie-down at the entrance."

Dalton and Jacob quickly backtracked to the house. Dalton gathered up the rope and slid the coil over his shoulder. They re-entered the mine, securing one end of the rope to a timber framing the door. Dalton slid loops of rope off his shoulder as they descended, stringing a line down the center of the adit shaft. With their escape route marked, Dalton and Jacob breezed assuredly past the side-shaft, fifty feet in.

The boys quickly discovered the mine was riddled with diverging drift shafts. Tunnels of various sizes and states of repair jetted off from the main shaft every twenty or thirty feet. The door in Dalton's cellar had led to a kind of subterranean labyrinth.

Dissected as it was, the heart of the main shaft ran relatively straight into the mountain. Dalton counted the sets of wooden supports as they descended. "That's twelve" he said, "we must be about a hundred and twenty feet in."

"Probably right," Jacob replied, "that rope's a two-hundred-footer; looks like we've used a little more than half."

By the time they passed the seventeenth set of supports, the remaining rope around Dalton's torso was light. His conscience, on the other hand, was weighing heavy. "Let's head out," he said, suddenly.

"What's up?" Jacob said.

"My parents will be home soon," Dalton said. "They're scared to death of mines. We really have no business being in here."

Jacob knew Dalton was right, but considering how far they'd come, he didn't see any reason not to go to the end of their safety line. It was only thirty feet more. "I hear you," he said, "but we only have a little bit of rope left. Let's play it out. We aren't in any danger."

Dalton ignored his friend's reasoning. "That's all for me, Jacob," he said. "Let's go." He turned up the shaft and started to gather up rope.

Jacob conceded, but couldn't resist shining his light down the abyss one final time. "Dalton, I think I see something," he said.

Dalton stopped and turned. He stepped to his friend and raised his flashlight, tracing Jacob's beam to an anomaly in the narrow void. A scattering of light-colored objects stood out against the surrounding dark rock and decaying wood. "What is it?" Dalton said.

Instinctively, the boys headed deeper into the adit, Dalton laying out the last of their rope.

"That's it," Dalton said, "two-hundred-feet, we're out of rope."

"It can't be fifty feet more," Jacob said. "One of us should go. You stay here and light my way. I'll be fine."

"Ok, Jacob," Dalton relented, "let's check it out, but I'll go." He handed Jacob the end of the rope and took off before his friend could object. "It's my basement," he shouted over his shoulder, smiling.

The mine seemed more primitive in its deeper recesses. Fallen rocks made the footing treacherous. Dalton glanced back every few steps. The glare of Jacob's flashlight was reassuring.

Jacob could see his partner was mere feet from the strange objects. "Can you see anything?" he shouted.

"Jacob," Dalton yelled, "it's bones, maybe human."

Jacob abandoned the end of the rope and moved to join Dalton at the discovery. Dalton held what appeared to be the femur bone of a large mammal. Other bones lay at their feet, with many more strewn down the mine. They began looking diligently for a skull, anything to positively identify the remains.

Finding nothing concrete, Dalton began to question his original theory, "You know," he said, "these are probably elk bones. The carcass was probably drug in here by wolves or coyotes through a vent shaft, or before this house was even built." He stared at the large specimen in his hands.

Jacob, on the other hand, was leaning toward Dalton's initial idea. He'd helped his dad field-dress and butcher a lot of game, come across plenty of dead animals in the wilderness in his life. As a group, these bones didn't match anything he'd seen. "Let's gather up what we can and take them to the authorities," Jacob said. "Let somebody else figure it out."

"No," Dalton replied, "if they're human, the cops are going to want to see them right where they are."

"You're right," said Jacob, "but we're going to look like damn fools if we drag the sheriff down here to show him the skeleton of a yak, or some other critter."

Dalton knew he was in deep. "Well," he said, "let's just take this one bone and get it identified. If it's nothing, we'll pitch it in the woods. Then all I'll have to deal with is telling my parents there's a mineshaft in their basement, I blew a hole through their wall, and that I went in contrary to their instructions." He directed his light toward Jacob. "Where's the rope?" he said, realizing neither of them was holding the safety line.

"I had to leave it to get to you," Jacob said. "The rope wasn't long enough."

The boys simultaneously turned and pointed their lights up the mine. The rope stood out clearly on the rock floor. They knew they'd dodged a bullet. They exited the mine and carefully hid the wooden door, strategically placing moving boxes behind the stair slats.

Dalton and Jacob took the bone to Dalton's room, speculating over the relic's nature and pondering their next move. They agreed the specimen needed to be identified. But finding someone with expertise and discretion was a monumental challenge. They pondered Jacob's family doctor, the local veterinarian, an anonymous submission to a university, even the grocery-store butcher in Montrose. But no one, nothing, made sense. They decided to sleep on it.

Dalton barely slept a wink. The next morning, he was still trying to come up with a candidate to help identify the bone from the mine. Truth was, he was leaning toward telling his parents the whole story. He would take his medicine and allow them to make the next call. Still, he couldn't make that decision without talking it over with Jacob. Dalton was brushing his teeth when the perfect person came to mind, his high school biology teacher.

Michelle Stipple was a young science instructor at Jefferson High and perhaps the least tenured teacher at the school. She was also, far-and-away, Dalton's favorite. Miss Stipple had a way of making even the most tedious material interesting. Dalton found her enthusiasm contagious. But it wasn't Stipple's teaching ability that made her the perfect candidate in Dalton's mind. It was a judgment she'd made, and a kindness she'd shown him.

It happened on Dalton's third day at the school. He'd never been in serious trouble at Jefferson or any other place for that matter, but Miss Stipple couldn't have known that. Someone had been smoking in the restrooms. Dalton's locker was situated between the boys' and girls' facilities, and he'd noticed the smell of smoke. The school's assistant-principle had made an announcement on the first day of class, reminding students of a mandatory suspension that would be metered out to anyone caught smoking or vaping on school grounds. Monitors had been making random checks on the restroom facilities, but Dalton hadn't heard of anyone getting caught.

On that morning, after a crush of kids had visited the surrounding double-stacked lockers, Dalton was left alone sorting his books. Michelle Stipple cleared her throat in a way people do to get someone's attention. Dalton's eyes met her gaze and followed it down to the ground near his feet. A pack of cigarettes lay immediately beneath his locker. Miss Stipple must have sensed the innocence in Dalton's reaction. Rather than reprimand him, she picked up the smokes and slid them discreetly into her lab coat. She motioned Dalton into her class.

At the end of the period, Stipple asked Dalton to stay for a minute. She waited for the other students to exit before addressing the situation. Dalton began to plead his case before she had a chance to talk. "Dalton, relax," she said, "I believe they're not yours. I just wanted to ask you where you moved here from, how things are going."

From that day on, Dalton had the upmost respect for his teacher. He believed in his heart that Miss Stipple would use discretion about the bone, and where he and Jacob had found it.

D alton glanced at himself in the living room mirror before heading for the bus. The concealed bone disproportionately stretched his backpack to its limits. *"So much for being inconspicuous,"* he thought.

Jacob hustled up behind Dalton on the street as the pair headed toward the bus stop. "Looking for the bell tower, Quasimodo?" he said.

Dalton removed the pack and grabbed it briefcase-style, minimizing the bag's distorted shape. Somehow, he managed to make it to school, and then his locker, without provoking any more comments or questions.

Dalton and Jacob devoured their lunch in minutes that day. They grabbed the bag containing the bone from Dalton's locker and headed toward the science lab. Miss Stipple was just finishing her meal when the boys knocked and opened the door.

"Miss Stipple," Dalton said, "can we speak to you a minute?"

Jacob stood a half step behind.

"Of course, come in," Michelle replied.

"We found something, and we need help figuring out what it is," Dalton said, his hand trembling as he pulled the bone from his backpack.

"Where did you find that?" Miss Stipple said, before Dalton could place the bone on the desk.

The tone in Michelle's voice told Jacob she had the same impression he did; it was a human leg bone. He didn't know the science teacher as well as Dalton. He began to wonder if they'd made a mistake. "We just happened across it," Jacob blurted out.

"—in a mine," Dalton continued.

Jacob was surprised by Dalton's frankness, but was relieved to be taken off-point. He braced for Miss Stipple's response.

"Where?" Stipple asked, sounding shocked. "What were you guys doing in a mine?" She spoke in an authoritative tone Dalton wasn't expecting.

"Well, we—," Dalton stammered, "—I mean, we know we shouldn't have been in a mine, but that's another story. Anyway, we found some bones, and we were afraid they might be human. On the other hand, we didn't want to make a fuss if they were from an animal. We decided we needed a person we could trust, and we chose you."

Michelle Stipple stared at Dalton, reading him. She then turned to Jacob, regarding him briefly through a stern squint. Finally, she turned her attention back to the bone specimen. "Well," she began, "this is no fossil. It's dry, but recent. Definitely the femur of a mammal."

In her mind, Michelle was ninety-nine percent sure of what she was looking at, but she stalled to sort her thoughts. "Let's look at a reference book," she said, turning toward a bookshelf.

"I think it's human," Jacob said. "I've never seen a harvested animal or buzzard-cleaned carcass like this, and I've seen everything that roams Colorado."

Dalton shot Jacob a menacing look before quickly addressing their teacher. "We don't know what it is, Miss Stipple," he said. "That's why we brought it to you."

"Jacob, I tend to agree with you," Michelle said. "This looks like a human femur, the large bone of the upper leg. Here's an anatomy book." She grabbed the textbook from the shelf.

Dalton was sorting his thoughts. On one hand, he was horrified they'd apparently found human remains. On the other, he was glad to know what they were dealing with. It was a comfort to have Miss Stipple involved.

Michelle laid the large book on the desk and quickly fanned through its contents. Printed paper gave way to transparent plastic pages with colorful graphics, systems of the human anatomy, each subsequent transparency ascending deeper into the human body. The final page showed the skeletal system. She traced the image of the femur bone on the page with a retracted pen, alternately looking at the book and the physical specimen, comparing their respective shapes and proportions. There was no questioning the similarities. "Guys, I'm pretty sure this is human," she concluded. "Now, please tell me where and how you found it."

Dalton explained how they'd found the mine-door in his cellar, and how curiosity had gotten the better of them.

Michelle told them that she had recently read about an incident where coyotes dug up a cemetery in Wyoming, desecrating the graves. She theorized the same thing might have happened in Lobos. She, nevertheless, gave the boys strict instructions, "Take the bone to the sheriff's office. Tell them exactly what you told me."

Dalton and Jacob nodded in agreement.

"In the meantime, I have to report this to the administration," Michelle said.

"Can you please wait?" Dalton said. "Even you said you can't be one-hundred percent sure what it is."

"I'll give it a couple days," she said, "but talk to the sheriff. And you need to tell your folks."

The boys promised her they would.

Chapter 12

Good Morgan

Dalton knew before he left Miss Stipple's classroom his promise to speak with the sheriff and his parents about the bone and the mine would have to wait a day. He had important plans for that afternoon; Cheyanne Connery was paying a visit to Lobos. Despite the teens' daily bus rides, hallway talk, and extensive texting, the afternoon would be Dalton and Cheyanne's first real personal time together outside of school. The plan was for Cheyanne to get off at the Lobos bus stop with Dalton. Cheyanne's mother would meet them, and Susan Wallace, at the Wallace residence for a snack, then give Cheyanne a ride home after the two moms had a social visit. The kids would have a couple of hours together before the Connerys returned to Querido for the dinner shift at their restaurant.

Dalton was excited but a little anxious about Cheyanne's visit. Even though he'd grown comfortable talking to her on the bus and in the halls, most of their more intimate communications had been cloaked by their phones and social media. The idea of carrying on a physical conversation, lasting for hours, made Dalton apprehensive.

The ride home on the bus that afternoon was normal enough. Jacob and Jimmy gave the couple their space and went their own ways after they unloaded in Lobos. Jacob had put the mysterious bone in his pack for the ride home, anticipating his friend's afternoon plans.

When Dalton and Cheyanne got to the Wallace residence, Susan was upstairs readying herself. A simple but attractive setting for four was assembled on the kitchen table.

"Something smells good," Cheyanne said as they walked in.

Dalton immediately heard a car pull up outside and looked out to see Cheyanne's mother coming up the walkway. He had already invited her in when Susan Wallace joined them in the foyer.

"Hello," Susan said to Mrs. Connery. "And hello to you too, Cheyanne. Welcome. I was just about to pull a cake out of the oven."

The two moms were acquainted, although their interaction had been limited to short, superficial conversations in the pizzeria in Querido. The ladies sensed a good chemistry, and their children's budding friendship was a good excuse to get together.

The four Coloradans sat down at the kitchen table. Dalton poured himself a glass of water from a pitcher and started toward the cake. Susan caught her son's eye, stopping him cold.

"Oh, yes," Dalton said. He sat the knife down and asked their guests what they wanted to drink. He filled the remaining glasses with water and disappeared into the kitchen. When he returned, Susan had cut and served four pieces of cake. Dalton placed a single candle in Cheyanne's slice and ignited it with a lighter. "You never told me about your birthday," he said.

Cheyanne blushed and blew out the candle. "My bad," she said.

"Better late, than never," Dalton said.

Mrs. Connery complimented Susan on a delicious cake and Susan beamed. "That means a lot coming from a successful restaurateur, like yourself," she said.

The youths finished their snack and Dalton asked if they could be excused. The ladies were busy conversing and sipping their coffee. Susan nodded her consent.

Dalton and Cheyanne walked out the front door to an especially pleasant fall afternoon. After Dalton introduced Cheyanne to Breitling's and picked up a pack of gum, the pair started a walk down the valley. They strode through lush grass near the highway shoulder past the structures and clearings of town to where the basin narrowed, and the mountains jutted abruptly upward. When they'd reached the end of the valley, Dalton suggested an alternate route back; a trail that traced the base of the mountains, opposite his home. "It's safe and tame," he said, reassuring Cheyanne.

Cheyanne had changed into her hiking shoes on the bus and was eager to explore. "Let's do it," she said.

The path along the Lobos valley edge started out wide. Saplings and young trees sporadically lined the trail, diffusing sufficient sunshine to warm the hikers and green the late-season grass. The trail followed the mountain face, veering from the developments of town, tracing the mountain ridges and outcrops that jutted into the valley. After a short distance, the path began to narrow and entered a grove of Aspens. Dalton pointed to a set of deer tracks in the moist soil. "That's how the trail was made," he said. "But it definitely circles back to town; I've been here plenty of times."

The further Dalton and Cheyanne hiked, the narrower the path became. Underbrush and small trees leaned over the path until there was no longer room to walk side-by-side. Dalton took the lead, looking back frequently to see if Cheyanne was keeping pace. He crossed a rocky creek bottom, its flow too shallow for minnows. He feared Cheyanne might be getting anxious about their isolation and turned casually to reassure her.

Before Dalton could speak, Cheyanne inexplicably turned upstream in the gulley. "Come on," she called out over her shoulder.

Even in its small pools, the stream's discharge barely overran the soles of the teenagers' shoes. Still, the moss-covered stones were slick as ice; it took everything Dalton had to keep from slipping. He was amazed by Cheyanne's balance and agility as she moved effortlessly over the smooth rocks. Their trek came to an abrupt halt where the creek reached the valley's edge and the mountain ascended. The stream disappeared into a fissure in the rock face.

Dalton caught up to Cheyanne, looking intently into the void.

"What is it?" Cheyanne asked.

"I don't know," Dalton said, "probably just a deep crevasse. Could be a cave." He'd never ventured up this particular creek.

"Let's take a look inside," Cheyanne urged.

"Probably not a good idea," Dalton said. "It's dark and my phone light is broken." He hoped Cheyanne would press. The cavern would be intimate. Still, he didn't want his wishes to be misinterpreted.

"Let's just go in as far as we can see," Cheyanne urged. "Anyway, I have a light." She handed Dalton her phone, its strong flashlight already illuminated.

Dalton went through the crevasse first, his shoulders and hips turned sideways to squeeze between the rocks. Cheyanne came in more easily, but even her small frame blocked most of the light as she breached the cave's narrow opening. Inside, they found a more generous space, a walk-in closet sized cavity. A smaller, adjoining cavern lay opposite the entrance. Water showered down into the littler cave from somewhere inside the mountain, crossing the floor at Dalton and Cheyanne's feet. Dalton bent down with

Cheyenne's light to peer into the smaller opening. The low cave continued in another five feet before turning decisively upward from where the water fell into the truncated space.

Dalton handed Cheyanne her phone and rested on a stone protruding from the cave wall. Cheyanne found a ledge to sit on and extinguished her light. In the dim light creeping through the cave entrance, Dalton thought he saw Cheyanne smile. He wondered if it was because of their odd environment, but hoped it was because they were together, alone. He wanted to move close, thought how much he would like to kiss her. But there were so many potential problems with that. For one, he was nervous. Secondly, he wasn't sure she wanted him to do it. In any event, an approach would be awkward in the dark and cramped cave.

For her part, Cheyanne wanted the kiss. She had thought about their first kiss a lot. She anticipated this might be the day.

Insecurities got the better of Dalton and he gave up on his romantic idea. He felt the silence becoming awkward and moved toward the cave exit. "Let me go out first," he said. "I'll give you a hand."

Cheyanne was seated closer to the cave mouth and moved to allow Dalton through. As she brushed by him, beams of direct sunlight penetrated the opening. A strange reflection on the ground caught her attention. "Dalton look," she said. She reached down to the rock floor.

Before Dalton could react, Cheyanne had picked up a round silver object. Even in the limited light of the cave, she immediately recognized the discovery, a silver dollar.

Dalton took a knee and began sweeping away debris, looking for more coins. Within seconds, he found a second silver dollar in nearly the same spot. Cheyanne engaged her flashlight and bent over, sifting the sand and rock with her free hand. Almost instantly, she recovered a third coin. They bore down together, moving loose stones and soil, working from the cave's center toward the perimeter. In a matter of minutes, they'd found six shiny silver dollars in total.

Cheyanne shined her light into the lower, smaller cavity of the cave. She saw the upturned tunnel and small pool of water, but no sign of additional coins. Just as quickly as it had begun, Dalton and Cheyanne's silver rush was over.

Treasure in hand, the pair climbed out of the cave, breathing heavily from their frantic work and excitement. In the light of day, they stared at each other in amazement. Cheyanne knelt to wash the sand from the coins in the tiny stream, handing them up to Dalton one by one. Dalton studied the coins diligently. They were all nineteenth-century Morgan dollars, solid silver.

"How did they get here?" Cheyanne said.

"Hidden or lost, I guess," Dalton said. "Probably by miners. A dollar was a lot of money back then." He handed Cheyanne their treasure.

Cheyanne felt the weight of the heavy coins, observing their glimmer. "Seems like a lot of money right now," she said, her eyes beaming. "They're awfully shiny for having been in a cave for a hundred years."

As Dalton and Cheyanne retraced their steps down the creek to the trail, Dalton speculated about the origin of the cave. "The waterflow is probably much higher in springtime and the early summer when the snow melts. The runoff probably works its way down through the cracks. The cave was probably formed by erosion over tens, or even hundreds of thousands of years." He suddenly stopped talking. *Cheyanne probably knows all of this,* he thought.

"That's interesting," Cheyanne said, "but I'd love to know why anyone would put silver coins in a place like that."

"I agree," Dalton said, nodding.

As certain as Dalton was about the cave's origin, he was less sure about the history of the coins. The pieces they'd found were bright and shiny, in excellent condition. The few silver coins he'd collected over the years were dark and tarnished. The only place Dalton had ever seen silver shine so brilliantly was in a coin shop. Those pieces had been sealed and protected immediately after their minting.

As they reached the main trail, Dalton had an idea. "We have twenty minutes," he said. "Let's backtrack, take the easy way back to town and stop by the antique store. They sell coins. Maybe the guy who runs the shop can tell us more about the Morgan dollars."

"Sounds good," Cheyanne replied.

"One thing," Dalton cautioned, "we need to do this without giving the store owner any ideas about where these coins came from. Jacob is uncomfortable with the guy."

Dalton and Cheyanne retraced their steps along the game trail until they reached the wide-open meadow of the valley. Dalton slowed down as they reached the clearing and fell back toward Cheyanne. They strolled side by side, passing the coins back and forth, excitedly recounting their amazing experience in the cave. Dalton fumbled one of the silver dollars to the ground and the pair simultaneously bent down to grab it. Cheyanne's reflexes were quicker; her slender fingers quickly enveloped the coin hidden in the grass. Dalton's grasp fell over Cheyanne's loose fist. He held on firmly as the two stood up. The Colorado teens intertwined fingers and walked hand-in-hand into Lobos' business district.

The couple found the antique store unoccupied, as Dalton had on his first visit. Dalton let go of Cheyanne's hand and pulled the door open for her. The anvil doorstop lay several feet inside the store, tucked up against the shop's front wall. Dalton marveled at the force it would take to move the heavy object such a distance and wondered why anyone would bother to do it. *"Thus, the forearms,"* he thought, finally.

"Hello, anybody here?" Dalton said.

Dalton and Cheyanne walked over to the coin counter together and waited for the shopkeeper. As Cheyanne looked through the glass countertop, she couldn't help thinking there wasn't anything as impressive there as what she had in her pocket.

Horrance Taber descended the stairs and entered the room. "Yes?" he said.

"Hello Mr. Taber," Dalton said, pulling a silver dollar from his pocket. "We have a coin we'd like to learn about."

Cheyanne gripped the Morgan dollars in her jeans' pocket as she moved to Dalton, ensuring the coins didn't clank or jingle.

"There must be some confusion," Taber said. "This is a store, not a museum."

The man's comments were obviously condescending, but Dalton was determined to take advantage of the shopkeeper's knowledge. "Well," he began, "I'm sure you're an expert; would you mind at least taking a look?"

Taber reluctantly accepted the coin, examining it briefly. He stretched out his hand, offering it back. "A nineteenth-century Morgan dollar," he said. "It's old, but common. "I'll give you $15 for it."

Dalton hadn't considered selling the coin but was intrigued by Taber's offer. He thought about Jacob's suspicion about the man and assumed the shopkeeper was starting negotiations low. When Dalton and Jacob had sold their panned gold in Grand Junction, they also learned silver was trading at more than $25 an ounce, the exact weight of the coin.

"No thanks, Mr. Taber," Dalton said, turning to lead Cheyanne out of the store. "We appreciate you taking a look, though."

"$20," Tabor hedged, "that's all it's worth. Like I said, it's common, not worth more than its metal."

Dalton was curious how much the coin was really worth and walked back toward the counter. He'd noticed a coin collector's publication he was familiar with on a table behind the shopkeeper. The book showed values of most U.S. minted coins. "Can I see that?" he asked, motioning toward the reference. "If you don't mind."

Tabor grimaced and reluctantly handed Dalton the periodical. Dalton scanned the Morgan dollar section for the date and mint designation on the coin. Tabor was right about the commonness of the piece, hundreds of thousands like it had been minted, but he failed to consider the coin's excellent condition.

Dalton studied the definitions of coin condition and the price table for the piece in his hand. I'd say this coin rates, at minimum, extra-fine, Mr. Taber. This book says it's worth $30-$35."

Tabor knew from the moment he'd seen the Morgan dollar the coin was in pristine shape. "I'll give you $25 for it," Taber conceded. "The numbers in the book are retail. I need a mark-up. I'm not running a non-profit."

Dalton understood he and Cheyanne hadn't discussed selling any of their treasure. "What do you think, Cheyanne?" he asked.

"Let's do it," she said. "We can use the money for a movie or dinner."

Dalton handed Taber the Morgan dollar. The antique dealer placed the coin in the glass case in front of him and pulled three crumpled bills from his dirty trousers, handing them to Dalton.

As they left the store, Dalton immediately began thinking about the date Cheyanne suggested.

Chapter 13

Rushed Business

Sheriff Buford gazed at his image in an antique dressing mirror in the corner of his Lobos office. The lines on his face synchronized with the cracking paint on the wall behind him. His trousers were one broken belt away from dropping to the ground. The young and fit deputy of decades past had been supplanted by a middle-aged man besieged by weight gain and dogged by arthritis. His shoulders ached as he struggled to cover his bald dome with the long hair on the side of his head.

The annex building showed more wear than the sheriff himself. Water dripped from multiple locations below the sink in the office's tiny bathroom. The toilet had to be flushed via direct pull on the flapper; each trip to the head required a hand dip into frigid water to retrieve the metal chain. The temperature inside the office was rarely comfortable. The heat was provided by an electric space heater. Air-conditioning had never been installed. Buford had included renovations in his annual budget submission, but it wasn't approved. His emergency requisitions for repairs had been ignored. Still, he preferred the solitude of Lobos to his main office in Ouray.

Buford tightened his belt down a safety notch and exited the office, bolting the annex door with a key. He walked briskly across the street to the antique store operated by Horrance Tabor. Ignoring the store's *closed* sign, he passed through its unlocked door.

Taber was used to Sheriff Buford's unannounced visits, but this one was especially annoying. He heard the sheriff's bellow from the floor below, but his own voice wasn't strong enough for Buford to hear. "I'm coming," he shouted repeatedly.

Sheriff Buford had seen Taber's minivan parked outside. When the shopkeeper didn't immediately present himself, the sheriff figured he might be busy. He straddled a stool at the counter, looking at the showroom and merchandise. "*What a pathetic excuse for a store*," he thought.

Buford was tired. He closed his eyes and placed his elbows on the counter, entwining his fingers, balancing his forehead on uplifted thumbs. The commode flushed above and Buford perked up. The store's lackluster coin assortment laid immediately beneath a glass counter where he sat. Something new caught his eye.

The shopkeeper immediately emerged from the staircase, entering the room. Taber's pale brow was running with sweat from rushing his business, his stringy salt-and-pepper hair shiny from poor hygiene.

"Dropping the kids off at the pool?" the sheriff asked, chuckling.

Taber sat down nervously on a couch near the front window of the smoke-filled shop, his muscular forearm hanging over the sofa clutching a cigarette. The ash tray next to him desperately needed emptying and the filterless smoke he was working on burned low near his fingers.

"Horrance, how's it going?" Buford asked. "You've been staying out of trouble, I'm sure."

"Sure, Sheriff," Taber replied, "same old, same old." He drew a drag from his cigarette.

"You sure?" Buford said. "I can always check with your parole officer."

"Don't forget," Taber began, "the state probably wouldn't approve of a parolee living so close to his arresting officer."

Buford considered Taber's comment and was silent.

"How's business?" the sheriff asked, finally, knowing full-well that shoppers in the store were rare.

The nervous shopkeeper's cigarette reached his cuticle, stinging him sharply. He dropped the smoke, extinguishing it with his heel. "Seriously sheriff," he said, "how does the state expect me to make a living here?"

Buford looked at Tabor in disgust. "If you think the state is stingy, you ought to check out the county government," he said. "Now, show me this silver dollar in the cabinet." The sheriff was pointing.

Taber got up and fumbled nervously with the cabinet latch. He handed the coin to the sheriff.

Buford examined the piece. "Morgan dollar," he said. "A rare one?"

"No," Taber replied, "common as a sparrow. But in excellent condition."

"This is a step up for you, Horrance," the sheriff said. "Where'd it come from?"

"I bought it from the new kid in town," Taber conceded. "And some girl."

Buford stood up and handed Taber back his coin. "Well, hopefully you'll make some money off of it," he said. "It certainly seems like you need it."

Chapter 14

Connecting the Rocks

Dalton was having an especially hard time getting out of bed for school. After Cheyanne and her mom had left the previous afternoon, he did homework until near midnight. He was wishing he'd taken advantage of the previous weekend to get ahead on his schoolwork. Instead, he was cramming on long-term projects while trying to keep up with his daily assignments. He pried himself out of the sack and showered.

As he got dressed, Dalton considered his bigger problems. In addition to not getting with the sheriff the previous day as Miss Stipple instructed, his parents were still in the dark about the mine. His mom left daily on an early schedule for work, but his dad was sometimes home when he left for the bus. He stepped to the top of the stairwell of their two-story home, peering down. The smell of coffee and toasted bread pervaded the air. Dalton descended the stairs slowly, considering how he'd tell his dad he'd ventured into a mine, and that the chasm behind their house might contain a human body.

Downstairs, the curtains were open and natural light flooded the house. Dalton looked out at the drive. Both of his parents' cars were gone; his father had already left. Dalton was at once relieved and apprehensive. His shocking revelations weren't going to happen that morning, but he would have to deal with his stress over their repercussions another day.

Dalton climbed the stairs to his bedroom, anxious and tired. Despite his weariness, he finished his morning routine with a few minutes to spare. As had been his habit during the carefree mornings of summer, he walked to the large window in the front of his bedroom to look for wildlife on the adjacent mountain.

The elevation of Dalton's second story window added immensely to his perspective. He could see the hiking trail Cheyanne and he traversed days earlier, but the creek bed between the trail and the cave was hidden by dense foliage. He wondered if his new scope might draw him in close enough to see the fissure.

Dalton grabbed a toolbox from his closet and unlocked his safe. He pulled out his hunting rifle and painstakingly detached the scope from the gun. He slid the firearm back into the locker. Detached from his rifle, the sight had the basic form of an old-fashioned telescope, but its sleek aluminum body gave it a high-tech edge and made it light as a feather. The sight's oval lens flashed a menacing squint from the front.

Placing the device in front of his eye, Dalton glassed the adjacent mountain. Although he'd used the scope dozens of times with his rifle, he was still amazed by its magnification and clarity. The treetops formed a shell over the edge of the valley and lower regions of the mountain. Dalton's view was opaque and green. He moved the sight back and forth across the dark canvass, looking for an opening or landmark. A small gap in the trees revealed a glistening of light. The unmistakable wakes of water bugs were visible in a pool. Dalton followed the break in the foliage to the mountain face. The cleft in the rock where they'd found the coins was clearly visible.

Dalton considered the possibility that the stream that flowed through the cave was a reemergence of a watercourse above. He decreased the scope's magnification for a wider view. He quickly lifted the front of the sight upward, looking for a significant spring, glacier, or snow-collecting bowl big enough to create waterflow capable of eroding a cave. The higher he raised the scope, the steeper and dryer the mountain face appeared. The trees quickly gave way to the high altitude and Dalton's lens was filled with rock. Within a few additional vertical degrees, he'd reached the top of the mountain. Only a few small patches of snow and ice nestled in narrow ravines were to be seen.

Checking his watch, Dalton realized he had less than ten minutes before the bus would arrive, insufficient time to re-install the scope on his rifle. He quickly closed the safe door in his closet, spinning the dial, securing the gun. He turned one last time to the adjacent mountain with the scope. Beginning where he'd left off on top of the ridge, he slowly lowered the sight across the wilderness. In the wide periphery of the oval lens, he spotted the bullet-riddled barracks of the Winning Stakes Mine.

Scanning the camp, the mine's crumbling waterwheel quickly came into view. A slow but steady stream flowed beneath its shattered paddles. Holding his position, Dalton once again dialed-up the magnification of the scope to 20x, drawing himself infinitely close to the watercourse. He traced the creek's flow below the camp's barracks through groves of small trees. Compact as it was, the stream swerved and fell between boulders and rock, zigzagging rapidly down the mountain.

In his haste, Dalton skipped ahead, losing track of the waterway. He drew the scope back slowly, looking for a familiar landmark. Three large boulders created a u-like shape, funneling the creek's flow, dropping it over their form to an invisible void. A hundred- and eighty-degree survey below the tiny falls failed to show a trace of the creek. It simply disappeared into the mountain.

Once again, Dalton adjusted his scope for a broader view. He carefully lowered the sight directly down the mountain from the three boulders. The cave where he and Cheyanne had found the coins lay a thousand feet directly below the disappearing stream.

Chapter 15

Three Hundred and Thirty Feet in

When Dalton arrived at school Tuesday morning, Miss Stipple was waiting by his locker. He had no illusions about her agenda. "Good morning Miss Stipple," he began, preemptively, "I need to tell you something; we didn't get a chance to talk to Sheriff Buford yesterday. Cheyanne Connery and I walked past his office twice, but we didn't see his car."

Dalton's explanation was technically true.

"Cheyanne Connery?" Michelle said, briefly pondering the implications. "Did you think about calling the sheriff? Does Cheyanne know about the bone you guys found?"

"No, she doesn't", Dalton said. "And that's why I didn't call him." Dalton knew what he said was a lie. Of course, Cheyanne didn't know about the bone. He didn't see any reason to complicate their relationship with the convoluted mess he'd found himself in, but he hadn't thought out the excuse about not calling the authorities until that very second.

"How about Jacob?" Miss Stipple continued. "Was it a double-date, or does he not have a phone?" As a rule, Michelle hated sarcasm, but given the circumstances, it was a preferable means to show her displeasure.

"It's something we want to do together," Dalton pleaded, "Jacob and me. We have nothing else going on tonight. I'm sure the sheriff will be around after school. If not, we'll call him, promise."

The bell rang and Miss Stipple and Dalton entered the classroom.

"Thank you again for helping us, Miss Stipple," Dalton said. "We won't let you down."

When the bus dropped Dalton and Jacob off in Lobos later that day, they skipped their usual raid on one or the other's refrigerator and proceeded directly to Sheriff Buford's office. Dalton was skeptical about the sheriff's presence. He saw Buford's empty parking place even before the bus came to a halt. Dalton and Jacob knocked on the door. Not surprisingly, there was no answer.

Dalton took out his cellphone to call the sheriff's office, but realized he wasn't sure how to do it. He knew 911 was going to get him an emergency dispatcher, but there was no immediate crisis. He opted for an internet search for a local number, the sheriff's landline. The phone link provided led to an electronic labyrinth of prompts, options, and bad on-hold music. "I'm not looking for the Higgs boson here," Dalton said, exasperated. "I just want to talk to a person."

Jacob could see his friend was frustrated. "Let's give Buford a little while," he said. "It's not even 3:30. He'll probably show up. If not, we'll call 911. We'll get it done today. Let's go test Miss Stipple's theory about animals digging up graveyards while we're waiting."

The cemetery in Lobos was tiny by any standard. Dalton and Jacob split up and walked the cemetery's two rows looking for any sign of disturbance. The marble and stone grave markers were covered with dirt and mold, most of them old and worn. Weeds invaded the plots, but aside from a few Ground Squirrel holes, everything was intact.

The boys walked back past the annex hoping to catch-up with the sheriff. His squad car was still absent. They walked to Dalton's house to get a snack. Susan Wallace had left a note for Dalton indicating she would be late and offering directions for reheating leftovers. His dad was on a three-day business trip to Utah.

As the microwave hummed, Dalton walked to the kitchen window. He could see the sheriff's vacant parking spot from his vantage point. "Let's go back in," he said.

"To the sheriff's office?" Jacob asked, fearing Dalton meant the mine, but not wanting to say it.

"I want to go back in the mine so we can prove to ourselves, to Miss Stipple, that this is nothing," Dalton said. "I have to believe those bones were drug into the mine by animals. I'm sure there's another way to get in, a vent shaft or something. So what if the cemetery isn't dug up, there must be settlers and

Indians buried all over these mountains. Besides, I'm willing to bet those other bones down there belong to a half-dozen animal species."

Jacob understood what his friend was saying, but he thought it was wishful thinking. He sensed Dalton was mostly stressed about his parents, what they would say when they found out about the mine. "You know," he began, "it's a thought, but we don't have the equipment for it. We only have a guide rope for two hundred feet, and we've been there, and beyond. It's too dangerous. We've done what we can."

"We don't need more rope," Dalton said. "The main shaft is fairly straight. With enough light, we can stay down the middle when we reach the end of the rope. We can count the support beams as we pass them. That way we'll always know where we're at. If our lights fail, we can work our way back along the side of the shaft to the two-hundred-foot mark—."

"—where we pick up the rope," Jacob said, finishing Dalton's thought. He was starting to understand Dalton's strategy, but there was still a disconnect. "What about the drifts, the side-tunnels? How do we account for those? We could turn down the wrong hole; somebody might find *our* skeletons one day."

"After two hundred feet, we won't go past any side-shafts," Dalton insisted. "We agree right now, not past one. If we come to a drift or split of any kind, we quit. We turn back."

Dalton waited patiently for Jacob's reply. "Agreed?" he said, finally.

"All right; let's do it," Jacob said. Heaven knew he also wanted the situation resolved.

Dalton grabbed the flashlights and rope while Jacob moved the boxes that blocked the entrance to the mine. Dalton saw an old backpack hanging on a hook and grabbed it. "We're going to need this to bring back the bones," he said.

As they entered the mine, Dalton checked his watch; it was 5:15pm. "My mom will be here by 8," he said. "We have less than three hours." Dalton slipped on the pack and fixed the end of the rope to a timber near the cellar door.

They started down the familiar route, playing their lights in front of them as Dalton laid out the rope. They passed the first side-shaft, fifty feet in. At two hundred feet, they reached the end of their safety line. Dalton laid down the end of the rope in the center of the adit and pointed at the adjacent wall supports. "Time to count," he said.

Jacob nodded in acknowledgment and took the lead, calling out numbers as they reached each support-set. Dalton repeated each number aloud, confirming their depth in the adit. They continuously scrutinized the continuity of the tunnel walls— Jacob the left, Dalton the right— looking for any side-shaft that would end their expedition. They couldn't take a chance of entering a side-tunnel.

Dalton let loose a whistle and pointed to the ground. They were entering the area of the bones. He picked up the first piece he came to and studied it. The sample was minute. *"Could be from a small animal,"* he thought. *"Or maybe a human finger or foot bone."* Dalton cringed.

Jacob tried to visually sort the specimens on the ground, looking for something unmistakably human. "How are we supposed to know what these things are?" he said. "Dalton, do you see the other femur?"

"No," Dalton said. "I can't remember exactly where I found the first one. Maybe we passed it. I can't see anything that I'd say is unequivocally human. You?"

"If I had to guess, I'd say most of this is people," Jacob said. "But who knows."

"Well, if they're human, there must be a skull. Keep looking," Dalton urged. "We need to go deeper."

"Got it," Jacob shot back.

Dalton and Jacob worked their way deeper into the chasm.

"Five," Jacob shouted, acknowledging the fifth set of mine supports since they'd reached the end of their safety rope, two hundred fifty feet in. He didn't remember the details of the deeper tunnel. He was surprised and pleased they hadn't encountered any side-shafts.

Dalton held up five fingers, repeating the call, confirming the count. He was on the opposite side of the adit from Jacob and moving fast. He approached the sixth set of supports in front of his friend.

Jacob observed the change in procession-order and worried they'd confuse the count. He sped-up to close the gap.

Dalton suddenly froze. "Stop," he cried out, realizing he'd kept his head down too long. He'd stopped looking for the side-tunnels.

What is it?" Jacob shouted back, his voice rising.

"Drifts," Dalton began. "I accidently quit looking. For at least fifteen feet."

"Shit, me too," Jacob said. "I got too focused on trying to catch up with you."

Dalton and Jacob stood motionless as they shined their lights on the mine walls behind them. The rock was uniform and incorrupt on both sides as far as their lights would reach. No intersecting side-tunnels were visible beyond two sets of supports, looking backward.

"That's twenty feet" Dalton said, relieved. "I know it wasn't further than that. We're okay. What's your count?"

"Next one makes seven since we laid down the rope," Jacob said. "I'm solid on that."

"That's what I got," Dalton replied.

The close call was exactly the type of confusion they were trying to avoid. At sixty feet from their lifeline, and two hundred and sixty feet from the exit, Dalton and Jacob couldn't afford to make a mistake.

Dalton pointed his light down the main shaft beyond where they'd reached. "Look, Jacob," he said. "Good thing we started paying attention."

Directly in front of them was a fork in the adit. Unlike the smaller, un-refined drifts that punctuated the first two hundred feet of the mine, the new adit was indistinguishable from the one they were in. There were now two main shafts.

"I guess we're turning back," Dalton said, stating the obvious.

"No doubt," Jacob replied. "But let's just inch-up to the fork and look. Let's throw some light down each of the tunnels and see what we can before we turn back."

They moved forward to a point where they wouldn't lose their orientation. Dalton inspected the right adit, Jacob the left.

"You see anything?" Dalton shouted.

"No, nothing. How about you?" Jacob replied.

Aside from a few fallen rocks, the adit Dalton inspected appeared just as the miners left it. "I don't see anything," he said. "Let's roll." But another idea immediately occurred to him. "Wait," he said. "Let's hit them together, double up the beams down each tunnel, get as much light as we can down there."

Dalton moved to Jacob. They crossed their light projections down his adit, playing their beams together, back and forth. Rock and brace timber extended as far back as their lights could reach.

They turned to Dalton's side, synchronizing their lights rhythmically down the tunnel.

Dalton and Jacob suddenly stopped their search, still as birddogs. Fifty feet down the shaft, several light-colored objects stood out against the dark floor.

"Oh man," Dalton said softly, "here we go again."

They decided they could precede safely using the system they had on the previous trip; one would move forward and the other stay behind to light the way. This time, Jacob would go.

"No matter what happens, Dalton," Jacob said, "stay right here. Your light is my ticket back."

"Got it," Dalton said, assuring his friend.

Jacob moved swiftly, motivated equally by curiosity and a desire to finish up and get out of the mine. He navigated through the rocks and crags, announcing his progress as he passed each set of supports. "That's eight . . . nine . . . ten . . .," he cried out.

Dalton sensed the sound of Jacob's voice growing fainter the deeper he descended into the mountain.

". . . eleven, . . . twelve—oh, God." Jacob's scream pierced the depths of the abyss.

Dalton knew something was terribly wrong. Jacob was sprinting in his direction without regard for the stones and debris in his path. Dalton's hands trembled as he tried to illuminate Jacob's way.

"Run," Jacob screamed, as he passed Dalton.

As Dalton ran in stride with Jacob, he tried desperately to keep his wits. He concentrated intently on the support timbers above, trying to keep track of their position relative to the safety line. ". . . six . . . five . . . four," he screamed.

They were almost to their lifeline. As they neared the two-hundred-foot mark, Dalton scanned the floor for the rope. He grabbed its end as he strode by, winding it around his arm. The primitive navigation system slowed him down. Jacob raced ahead.

Jacob burst through the cellar door and collapsed, rolling to a stop in the middle of the floor. Dalton followed close behind. He tossed the wound rope to the ground as he crossed the threshold, tripped over Jacob, and slid to the bottom of the staircase.

Jacob was finally able to articulate why he ran. "Ben Childress," he said, still panting. "He was face down, all messed up. But I'm sure it was him; we grew up together." Jacob rolled over and vomited.

Dalton helped his friend from the floor. "We have to call 911, now."

Chapter 16

Calling in the Law

The static in Dalton's ear dissipated as the 911 call dropped. "Shit," he said. "We need to get out of this basement and find some service." He led Jacob up the stairs, through the house, and out the front door.

"911," the operator finally said. "What's your emergency?"

The dispatcher's voice was barely perceptible, but Dalton knew the script. "Help us," he said. "We found our friend. He's been killed."

The dispatcher was having an even harder time hearing Dalton. "I can see you're calling from a cellphone. We have an extremely poor connection. What's your emergency?"

And the call dropped again.

Cell service was always sporadic in the mountains and the incomplete report wasn't uncommon to the emergency dispatch office. Despite an almost complete absence of conveyed verbal information, Dalton's call prompted a mobilization. State and county authorities in southwest Colorado were advised to standby for dispatch while technicians worked to identify the accessed cell tower.

Dalton and Jacob ran to the cemetery, the high point in the valley, desperate to use their cellphones. "Got one," Dalton said, finally picking up a bar.

Before Dalton could hit redial, the illuminated emergency lights of a squad car appeared at the edge of the valley. Dalton and Jacob quickly identified the vehicle as Ouray County Sheriff and ran to the middle of the street, intercepting the cruiser. They hunched over, hands on knees, gasping for breath. As the sedan came to a stop, they could see the driver was Sheriff Buford. His window was down and he was talking on the radio.

"Confirmed," Buford said into the chorded mic, "I have the 911 caller, will advise if assistance is needed." He racked his handset and climbed out of the car.

Dalton and Jacob began speaking excitedly over one another. The sheriff raised an open hand indicating it was time for the boys to be quiet. Like the day at the equestrian trail, Buford focused on Jacob with whom he was more familiar. "Jacob," he began firmly, "will you kindly tell me what's going on here?"

"We found a body, sheriff," Jacob said. "It's Ben Childress. In a mine." Jacob paused. He realized what he was saying sounded incredible.

"Where?" the Sheriff asked before Jacob could continue.

Dalton couldn't help from jumping in, "In the basement behind my house."

The sheriff turned toward Dalton, raising an eyebrow.

Dalton sensed the Sheriff's disapproval and fell silent.

Buford turned again to Jacob. "Continue please," he said.

"Ok," Jacob began, "We discovered an entrance to a mine in Dalton's cellar . . ."

"Mines again, Jacob?" the sheriff interrupted. "Haven't we discussed this?"

"I know," Jacob pleaded, "please hear me out. We went down in the mine a couple of times. We found a bone. The more we looked at it, the more we started to think it was human. We took it to school and showed it to our teacher. She thinks it came from a person. She told us to take it to your office, which we did today. But you weren't there."

"A bone? A bone you found." Buford said.

The sheriff's condescending tone seemed inappropriate to Jacob and Dalton, considering the circumstances.

"A bone is not dead people, Jacob," the sheriff continued. "How does your teacher know it came from a human? Did she do a DNA test on it? I didn't know they were that sophisticated over in Montrose County."

"The bone is nothing," Dalton interjected. "After we left your office, we went back down in the mine. Jacob went deeper than me, deeper than we'd been. That's where he saw Ben…" His voice trailed off. It was Jacob that had seen the corpse. Only he knew how convinced he was that it was Ben.

"You were on the right track earlier today," the sheriff said. "It's about time you got the law involved. Have you ever heard of a phone? Now, show me what you found."

The sheriff's radio chirped loudly. A dispatcher's voice followed. "Available units. Highway 62, two miles west of Ridgeway. Collision with injuries."

The sheriff turned to Dalton and Jacob. "I need to head over to Ridgeway," he said. "The State Police won't be able to get there for a while, I've got to handle this. I gather your parents aren't home."

Dalton nodded affirmatively. Jacob's mind had drifted back to the shocking image he saw in the mine. He stood motionless, staring at the ground.

"You two head back to Dalton's house," the sheriff said. "Stay there until I get back. There's no need to get folks excited about what you think you saw. I'll be back in an hour or so. We'll take a look together. In the meantime, stay out of the mine."

Buford climbed into his car and raced off without sirens or lights.

Dalton and Jacob turned and jogged back to the Wallace residence, neither of them expressing the anxiety they felt about moving back toward the carnage. They entered through the front door and headed up to Dalton's room without so much as a whiff of the door to the cellar.

Dalton immediately unlocked his safe. On a shelf next to his Browning and twenty-two caliber rifles sat a handgun he'd inherited from his grandfather. A training air rifle, a pellet gun from his childhood, sat propped up in the corner. He removed the pistol and prized Browning from the safe. "At this point, we can't take any chances," he said.

Jacob was amazed by Dalton's actions. He watched as his friend loaded the Browning rifle, set its safety, and propped it in the room corner.

Dalton then loaded five 357 rounds into the revolver and handed the pistol to Jacob. He reminded him that the gun had no safety. "Pull the trigger and it goes off," he said. He grabbed his rifle and took a seat on the edge of the bed.

A half-hour passed and Dalton and Jacob had barely spoken. Dalton grew more anxious. "My mom will be home in less than an hour," he said. "Where is Sheriff Buford?" He wondered which scenario was worse; his mom coming home before or after Buford's return.

Jacob interrupted Dalton's thoughts. "I have to go home. My parents must be wondering where I am. I'm going to tell them everything. Text or call me when Buford gets back."

"Ok," Dalton said. "But don't tell your parents about Ben unless you're absolutely sure it was him. You heard the sheriff."

"I know what I saw," Jacob said, flashing anger. "But I won't say anything. It won't bring Ben back, anyway."

"I believe you, buddy," Dalton said, looking down at the revolver in Jacob's hands. "Take it with you," he said.

"Thanks, but I'm fine without the gun," Jacob said.

Dalton looked intensely at his friend. "All right, then run your ass off."

Chapter 17

Abandoned

After Jacob left, it was painfully quiet in the house. Dalton sat nervously on the bed, his rifle across his lap, the pistol next to him on a pillow. He stared at a digital clock on his nightstand, marveling at how long a minute could last. The sun was long set, the twilight given way to a starry night. Through his window, Dalton could see moths swarm Lobos' two streetlights. He looked back at the clock, still unchanged.

Dalton thought of Cheyanne, what he might say if he could speak to her. He took his cellphone from his pocket. *"Finally, some service,"* he thought. He quickly typed out a text.

SOMETHING CRAZY'S HAPPENING. JACOB AND I FOUND A BODY. WE THINK IT'S BEN CHILDRESS. TALKED TO THE SHERIFF. CALL OR TEXT ASAP

Dalton hit send, and after what seemed like an eternity, the device signaled the message went through. Fifteen agonizing minutes past and there was still no response. *"Maybe her battery died,"* he thought.

It was past eight and Dalton's mother still wasn't home. For the first time in his life, he felt abandoned. Not by his mom or his friends, he understood everyone had responsibilities and distractions. Rather, it was a general sense of desertion, as if a veil of protection were suddenly lifted, leaving him to face his challenges alone. He touched his cross through his tee-shirt and looked down at his phone screen. One bar of service. He shot Jacob a text.

WHEN ARE YOU COMING BACK?

Jacob didn't answer. Dalton tried to call, switching to speaker phone. The phone rang several times before Jacob's mom picked up.

"Hello Dalton," Mrs. Burrell said.

"Hi Mrs. B. Is Jacob there?"

"No Dalton. I thought he was with you," she said. "But I can see he left his phone."

Dalton struggled not to show his concern. "He was on his way home when he left here a while ago," he said.

"Right," Mrs. Burrell said. "He was here. But he left back toward your place. I'm sure he's almost there. Tell him he forgot his phone, will you?"

"Of course, will do," Dalton said, relieved. "Thanks Mrs. B."

Dalton stored his weapons in his closet safe and went outside to wait for Jacob. He peered in the direction of his friend's house. Subtle lights from draped windows along the street permeated the moonless night. Jacob would be walking up at any moment. Dalton let loose a whistle, one he and Jacob frequently used when trying to be inconspicuous. He listened intently for a response. A cricket chirped annoyingly beneath the porch. He shouted Jacob's name through coned hands. There was only silence. *"He must have gone back to get his phone,"* Dalton thought. He sent another text.

COME BACK OVER HERE! WHERE ARE YOU?

Dalton went inside and back up to his room. Minutes passed and there were no messages from Jacob or Cheyanne. The gruesome discovery they'd made lay a few hundred yards from where he sat, and now he was worried about his best friend. He decided to walk to Jacob's house, and he was going to pick up an ally along the way, Jimmy Irwin.

Dalton could hear the laughing of children as he approached the Irwin residence. It was Jimmy's little sister and brother, four-year-old twins. Dalton calmed himself and caught his breath before ringing the bell. The ding sent the Irwin's Labrador into a frenzy. The little girl opened the door and leveraged all of her thirty-five pounds in the doorway to keep the dog from escaping. As she chased the pup back inside, the lab's wagging tail rapped her repeatedly in the face, all of which seemed to make her giggle harder.

Mrs. Irwin was working in the kitchen and stepped into eyeshot to see who their guest was. "Hi Dalton," she said, waving a dish towel.

"Hello, is Jimmy here?" Dalton replied. He squatted down in the entryway, scratching the dog's ears. He smiled at the twins, who were watching him intently.

"The boys are out back," Mrs. Irwin said.

"I'll go around," Dalton said. "No need to track dirt through the house." He prayed by *boys,* Mrs. Irwin meant Jimmy and Jacob. He rounded the corner of the house and fiddled with the fence latch. As he scanned the backyard looking for his friends, Dalton could see Jimmy's dad stoking flames in a firepit. He cleared his throat, announcing his presence, "Hello Mr. Irwin," he said. "Jimmy back there?"

Jimmy ducked out of the shed before his dad could respond. He walked past his father seated near the fire. His massive frame and the upward angle of the firelight created a sasquatch-like shadow on the outbuilding. "Hey Dalton," he said. "What's up?"

"Not much," Dalton hedged. "Just thought I'd stop by. Jacob here?"

"No, haven't seen him," replied Jimmy.

Dalton's heart sank, and anxiety began to pour over him like a wet blanket. He focused on the firepit, hoping Jimmy and his dad wouldn't notice his distress. He gathered himself. "Hey, you want to come over to my place?" he said.

"I do—," Jimmy said, hesitating, "—but I need to study. I'm taking the SAT again. I want to get into an honors program at college."

Dalton walked discreetly over to Jimmy and squared up in front of him, making sure he had his friend's full attention. He spoke in a nonchalant tone for Jimmy's dad's sake, but his expression was deadly serious. "How about just for a little bit?" he said.

At last, Jimmy perceived Dalton's urgency and need for discretion. "That okay with you, Dad?" Jimmy said.

Mr. Irwin consented without looking up from the fire.

Dalton led Jimmy through the gate and moved briskly across the yard. He was already two steps ahead of his friend when he started jogging. He yelled back at Jimmy, "Come on!"

Jimmy couldn't help but notice they were heading in the wrong direction, away from Dalton's house. He sprinted and caught up to his friend. "Hey Dalton," he said, "Where we going?"

"I'll explain in a minute," Dalton said. "Right now, we need to find Jacob."

Dalton and Jimmy stood in front of the Burrell residence. The car Jacob occasionally drove was parked out front. Dalton bypassed the front door and led Jimmy to a first-floor window. He crept up to the house and peeked inside.

"Are you crazy, Dalton?" Jimmy said.

"I hope so," Dalton said. "This will all be clear in a minute, bear with me." With Jimmy close behind, he circled around to the back of the house. He looked up at Jacob's dark, second-story bedroom window. "Not here," he sighed.

Dalton checked his phone for a text from Jacob. Nothing. "Let's go," he said, leading Jimmy to the street.

Jimmy grabbed Dalton's arm firmly, slowing him. "What's going on?" Jimmy insisted, breathing hard, visibly frustrated.

Dalton turned to his friend and stood still. "Jacob might have seen Ben Childress' body," he said. "He may be in trouble too. Let me explain . . ."

As Jimmy listened to the gruesome story about the discovery in the mine, he looked instinctively past Dalton's house to the Sheriff's Annex. The glare of a streetlight prevented him from seeing if Buford's squad car was parked out front. "This is just unbelievable, Dalton," he said. "Let's just pray Jacob is waiting in your living room."

Dalton's phone dinged. A text.

GOING TO BE LATER THAN EXPECTED. HOPE YOU ATE. LOVE YOU. MOM

Dalton and Jimmy sprinted to Dalton's house. They frantically called out Jacob's name as they rushed through the front door and swept through the rooms. Dalton led Jimmy into the kitchen. The cellar door was open. The single light mounted on the basement ceiling was illuminated. The boys stilled themselves in the silent house.

"Jacob," Dalton called down to the cellar.

There was no reply. No sound.

Dalton turned to Jimmy, collecting his thoughts. "Maybe Jacob showed up while we were at your house," he said. "Maybe he went into the mine to look for me."

"I know you two are good friends, Dalton," Jimmy said, "but I don't think Jacob would go into the mine alone unless he thought you were in trouble."

"You're probably right," Dalton conceded. "But what if he thought whatever killed Ben, got ahold of me."

"I don't know, Dalton," Jimmy said.

"Well," Dalton began, "I'm certain he wouldn't go into the mine without a guide-rope. Let's go downstairs and check. If our rope's there, we'll know Jacob didn't go in."

Dalton cautiously led Jimmy down the basement stairs. A sickening sour smell overwhelmed them.

"Good gracious, did somebody puke down here?" Jimmy said, pulling his sweatshirt over his nose and mouth.

"Yeah, I forgot to tell you about that," Dalton said, reaching up to open a foundation window.

Jimmy rounded the stairwell and squared up on the cellar wall and mine door. "This is incredible," he marveled, looking at the passageway. "Right here in your basement."

Dalton saw the rope where it had spilled from his arms. "Jacob's not here," he said, pointing. He led Jimmy around the casement, pausing on the stairs to look toward the sheriff's office through the open cellar window. The low angle obstructed his view.

"Let's go," Dalton said. "We need to call Jacob's parents. Hopefully, the sheriff's back, too."

Chapter 18

Through with Waiting

As Dalton and Jimmy headed upstairs, a faint but unmistakable cry resonated in the cellar. The sound clearly came from Jacob. Dalton and Jimmy froze on the stairs, listening for another clue.

Dalton felt as if a noose were suddenly tightened around his neck. Each swift and forceful beat of this heart sent blood to his brain that couldn't escape. "He's in the mine," he said, finally.

Jimmy looked out the open cellar window, puzzled by the direction of the sound. Acting on Dalton's hunch, he threw his muscular frame over the railing to the basement floor and yanked on the mine door, loosening its upper hinges from the doorjamb. He flipped on his phone light and started down the adit.

Dalton scrambled in behind Jimmy, grabbing the back of his friend's shirt. "Jimmy stop," he said. "It's too dangerous. We need help. We need to get the sheriff."

Dalton turned toward the dark tunnel. "Jacob," he screamed.

Jimmy followed Dalton's lead, shouting into the void. Their echoes returned unanswered.

Dalton and Jimmy ran from the house toward the Sheriff's Annex. The lawman's car was parked out front. They approached the office entrance, but the door was locked. Dalton peered through a window, finding a crack in a closed blind. The office was poorly lit. Papers were strewn across an untidy desk where a cup of coffee stood, steaming. But there was no sign of Sheriff Buford.

Dalton walked back to the road and leaned on Buford's cruiser. The engine's heat resonated in the sheet metal. "Where's the sheriff?" he shouted, bringing his fist down on the hood.

The small town center was dimly lit by a streetlight. Dalton and Jimmy moved quickly down Main Street, looking for the lawman. The windows of Breitling's store and the local implement dealer were dark. The only other illumination in the business district was at Horrance Taber's antique shop. They sprinted toward the store. Jimmy arrived first. He pounded on the door as Dalton peered through the window.

Taber slowly made his way to the front of the shop. "What is it?" he complained, unlatching the door, cracking it open.

"Sheriff Buford." The boys spoke over one another.

"We're looking for the sheriff," Dalton said, finally.

Taber grumbled further. "Well, he isn't here."

Dalton thundered all the louder, "Our friend is missing, Jacob Burrell. We need the sheriff, now."

Taber relented, opening the door wide, but blocking the entrance. "This is serious," the shopkeeper conceded. "But I don't know where the sheriff is." Taber observed the two young men a moment. "Why don't you go on home?" he said. "I'll keep watch for Sheriff Buford. When he comes back, I'll send him over to your house. It's the old Tucker place, isn't it?"

"Yes, thank you, Mr. Taber," Dalton said, leading Jimmy slowly back to the street.

Taber closed the door and locked the deadbolt.

Jimmy was visibly disturbed, shaking his head slowly. He wasn't at all satisfied with waiting for Sheriff Buford's return, let alone trusting the merchant to flag him down. He took out his cellphone. "I'm calling 911," he said, definitively.

Dalton nodded in agreement and started a slow jog toward home. Jimmy held the phone to his ear, trying to keep up, but it was impossible to keep pace and hear what was happening with the dispatch office. Dalton disappeared into the house just as Jimmy got connected.

"They're sending somebody out," Jimmy exclaimed, bursting through Dalton's front door. "They know what's going on."

The foyer and what Jimmy could see of the rest of the house were unoccupied. "Dalton?" he said, walking into the empty kitchen. He heard scratches, bangs and knocks coming from the cellar.

92

Dalton swiftly searched box after box, wildly discarding carton and contents with each fruitless inspection. His back was to the staircase as Jimmy reached the cellar. "Jimmy," he said without looking over, "I'm going in, you still game?"

"Of course," Jimmy replied. "But I got through. They're sending help."

Dalton turned to Jimmy, "I'm done waiting," he said.

Dalton found what he was looking for. He pealed open a package of batteries and loaded them into two flashlights. Handing one to Jimmy, he pointed at the coil of rope lying on the floor. "You carry that," he said. "Loop it over your head and shoulder. Here's a bottle of water. I have one too."

"That all we need?" Jimmy asked.

"Almost," Dalton said, handing Jimmy his loaded handgun. "I assume you know how to use this."

Jimmy tucked the gun under his belt.

Dalton's flashlight had an elastic strap designed to wear around the head. He positioned the lamp squarely on his brow. He wanted to keep his hands free for other purposes. He grabbed his Browning rifle and water bottle and moved toward the door.

As they started down the shaft, Dalton described the labyrinth of tunnels and their implicit danger, the rope system and spacing of supports. "The rope is our lifeline," he explained. "Last trip, we went in three hundred thirty feet, but the rope is only two hundred feet long. After two hundred, we start counting the old wooden support beams. There's a set every ten feet. The main shaft splits into two identical tunnels, down deep. Before that, there are smaller drift-shafts breaking off, leading to who-knows-where. The main shaft is fairly straight, though. We just need to stay down the middle of it, stay together, and concentrate. Disorientation will get us lost or killed."

Jimmy nodded.

The mine's low ceiling was not as forgiving to the big man as it had been for Dalton and Jacob. Projecting stones and broken, jagged rock draped unevenly above Jimmy's head. He pointed his light beam down the shaft into the void. Its glowing ray gradually expanded down the center of the tunnel but found no target within its visible reach.

Jimmy approached the first set of wooden supports. He observed the dark rock of the mine's walls and floor. Recently fallen debris cluttered the edges of the shaft. Loose, partially dislodged stones hung on the walls, hinged on their edges in mirrored cavities. As he bent down to pass under the support, Jimmy's heel landed awkwardly on a rock, rolling his ankle. He reflexively reached for the wooden beam on the wall. The rotten lumber crumbled in his powerful hand. He turned to Dalton as his friend looked on. He followed Dalton's eyes to the timber supporting the mine ceiling. "Now you know why I rejected the Colorado School of Mines offer, right off," Jimmy said.

"No doubt," said Dalton.

Twenty feet in, Dalton stopped, realizing no one knew where they were, where they were heading. He checked his phone, but there was no cell service in the mine. "Hold on Jimmy," he said. "Wait here, I need to leave a note." He raced back into the cellar, found a piece of paper and pencil, and quickly scratched out a message.

DOOR LEADS TO A MINE. JACOB IS MISSING. HAD TO GO IN.
SORRY. DALTON & JIMMY

He pinned the note on a rusty hinge-screw, still attached to the mine door.

As Dalton re-entered the tunnel, Jimmy let out a thunderous call for their lost friend. They stood still, holding their breath in silence, praying for an answer. Faint echoes returned in uneven volleys, but there was no sign of Jacob.

They started their trek down the shaft, Dalton on the left and Jimmy on the right. They scanned the adit floor, looking for any sign of their friend.

Fifty feet in, Dalton pointed to the first drift-shaft. It lay on Jimmy's side of the tunnel. "That's what we have to look out for," he said.

Dalton and Jimmy moved quickly past the dark side-tunnel, descending deeper and deeper into the mine. Jimmy laid out the rope, as instructed.

As they passed the eighteenth set of wooden supports, Dalton suddenly stopped. "Shit," he cried out.

"What is it, Dalton?" Jimmy said.

"My light is dimming," Dalton said, his heart racing. "I just put two new batteries in it. I can't believe it."

"Let's go back," Jimmy demanded.

"Can't," Dalton said. "If Jacob's down here, he needs us. Anyway, your light is strong, and I've still got some juice left. We have to keep going."

Jimmy had been silently counting the mine's support beams. He noted the nineteenth set and called it aloud.

"What are you doing, Jimmy?" Dalton asked, "We don't need a count until we run out of rope."

"It makes me feel better," he said.

Dalton couldn't argue the point and continued down his side of the adit.

Jimmy laid down the end of the rope within feet of the twentieth overhead support beam. He knew the rope was two hundred feet long and was amazed by the measuring accuracy of the old-time miners. He was even more surprised how vulnerable he felt letting go of the lifeline. "Twenty," he called out, his mouth growing dry.

"Now it gets really dangerous," Dalton said.

The lamp strapped around Dalton's forehead was nearly out. He worked his way over to Jimmy to share his light. "We're going to have to serpentine a bit," he said. "We need to cover every inch of the shaft, so we don't miss anything. You're going to see the bones we found, but ignore them for now."

"Where is Ben?" Jimmy asked, hesitating. "Where's his body?"

"At about three hundred thirty feet," Dalton said. "Hopefully, we'll find Jacob before we get that far."

Working with a single light, side by side, the trek was painstakingly slow. Dalton and Jimmy were now taking as many lateral steps as medial.

"Dalton," Jimmy said, "the bones are everywhere."

"I know, Jimmy," Dalton said. "Stay focused."

At wooden support set twenty-eight, they reached the fork in the main adit tunnel. Dalton and Jimmy were standing at the crossroads when all hell broke loose.

"Collapse," Dalton screamed.

Rock and timber rained down on the boys, violently knocking them to the floor, enveloping them.

Dalton lay motionless in the debris and dust, desperately trying to pull clean air into his lungs. He took inventory of his faculties. His legs and arms were free and moving but he couldn't get up. In the darkness, he didn't know which way was up. He felt heavy pressure on his back and abdomen. His chin was resting on his chest. The strain on his neck told him he was facing down. "Jimmy," he said, mustering a word with what breath he could gather. There was no answer. No sound.

Dalton pulled his elbows and knees to his torso to gain leverage against the mass that surrounded him. He hunched his back upward with all his might. The heap began to move. He gathered his strength and surged again. Stones and wood fragments tumbled. He struggled to his feet, only to stumble again, his equilibrium thrown off by the uneven ground and utter blackness. He reached out into the dark empty air calling for Jimmy. He reached what he presumed was the side of the shaft and turned sharply, bashing his head on a fallen boulder. "Damn it," he screamed, the pain surpassing what he'd experienced in the collapse.

Assuming all fours, Dalton turned slowly in the opposite direction, his arms alternately reaching out in front of him, searching for Jimmy and trying to avoid obstacles. He felt the smooth surface of a round stone in his path. He pressed it firmly, rolling the rock aside. The stone's light density surprised Dalton as he effortlessly swooshed the thing away. Sensing the object was manmade, Dalton reached out to recover it. He felt the article's form with both hands. With the sphere positioned between his palms, he probed its surface with his fingers. His pinkies slid into sequential voids, corresponding cavities on the sides of the orb. His thumbs disappeared into larger matching holes on the front.

"Skull," Dalton screamed, throwing the amalgamation of fused bones into the darkness. "Oh God, help us," he cried.

A faint groan filtered through the rubble directly beneath Dalton, Jimmy.

Dalton began digging. He metered his aggression as he worked his way toward the whimpers emanating from the heap, picking each rock cleanly to prevent shifts that might further injure his friend. He carefully reached into the evacuated area, searching for Jimmy's form. Probing the sides of the hole he'd made, his hand came to rest on a cold metal object. He pried it loose and felt its shape, Jimmy's crushed flashlight. He hit the switch, but to no avail. He felt the gap where the lens and bulb had been. He considered saving the batteries, but they weren't a match for his headlamp. Wherever it was.

Dalton continued to move rocks and splintered wood, listening carefully for his friend. He placed a two-hand grip on a large boulder, directly above where he'd heard Jimmy's cry. He positioned his body directly over the stone, flexed his knees, and lifted. As the rock gave way, he heard Jimmy violently draw in air. "Thank God," Dalton said. "Jimmy, it's me. You're going to be ok."

Dalton located Jimmy's head with one hand, his chest with the other, calculating the position of the rest of his body. He quickly removed what debris he could. Jimmy was unobstructed from the knees up, but a large timber laid across his lower left leg and foot. Dalton surveyed Jimmy's extremity above and below the fallen beam with his hands. His foot lay wedged beneath incalculable weight.

Jimmy was moving and becoming more vocal. Dalton couldn't make out his words, but it was clear his friend was in immense pain. Still, Dalton sensed

Jimmy's increased animation was a good sign. He made a final attempt to free his friend, digging under his foot. There was no soil to move, it was solid rock. Jimmy wasn't going anywhere.

There was no longer a choice, Dalton needed to go for help. But first, he needed to move Jimmy into a safe position. He moved behind his friend and grabbed him under the arms. "This might hurt a little, buddy," he said. "I need to make sure you can breathe." As he lifted Jimmy up straight, his scream was deafening. The trapped young man slumped over, motionless. Dalton placed his hand near Jimmy's mouth. He was breathing. He quickly finished moving his friend, taking advantage of his unconsciousness. He placed rocks and timbers on each side of Jimmy for support. Dalton felt his way to Jimmy's jeans pocket and slid out his cellphone. He probed the device for a flash or screen light, but the phone was ruined.

Dalton sat down next to his friend and gently patted him on the cheek, calling out his name. As Jimmy regained consciousness, he became anxious, trying to roll out of the seat Dalton worked so hard to arrange. Dalton put his arms tightly around his big friend's arms and torso, holding him in place. He uncapped his water bottle and placed it to his friend's lips. Jimmy took water into his mouth and swallowed. It seemed to comfort him. Dalton placed the water bottle in Jimmy's lap, positioning his friend's hands firmly around it. "I'm going for help," he said. "Your foot's stuck and I can't get you out. I'll be back soon, promise."

Jimmy uttered unintelligible words, but Dalton had already left his side.

Dalton crawled through the obscurity of the fallen rubble, his only marker the sound of Jimmy's labored breathing. He simply moved away. Each crawl-step brought a new bump or abrasion, heaping obstacle, or total obstruction. He moved about aimlessly, running into rock and shattered timber. He was certain he was going in circles. His sense of confinement by the restricted space was surpassed only by the total oppressiveness of darkness. It was as if Dalton was in a crypt, sealed by an immovable stone. He sank to the ground in despair.

Dalton heard Jimmy's faint voice in the stillness, the words indecipherable. "I'm going for help, Jimmy," Dalton called out. "I left you a water bottle. It's between your legs. Can you find it?"

"Twenty—"

Dalton heard Jimmy utter the number. He moved toward the sound of his voice. "What is it?" he asked, finally reaching his friend's side.

"Twenty-eight," Jimmy said, struggling. "We're at the twenty-eighth brace. Feel your way along the side of the mine back to the rope."

"You're right, Jimmy," Dalton said, with renewed hope. "I'm going. I'll be back for you soon."

Dalton combed the floor with both hands, moving forward in search of the rock wall, a guide back to the safety line. A warm feel of wood grazed his hand. Unlike the rough texture of the mine supports, this wood was dry and smooth. Dalton quickly recognized the stock of his Browning rifle. Miraculously, the gun had been thrown clear of the collapse. Dalton lifted it from the ground without clearing a stone. He slid the gun strap over his neck and shoulder and swung the rifle to his back, re-assuming all fours.

Dalton found the side of the shaft, stood up, and carefully began to move away from the debris field. A constant hand on the rock wall insured he would find the next wooden vertical support. He had no doubt it lay less than ten feet ahead.

Just as expected, Dalton found the beam. "*This is going to work,*" he thought.

Two support-sets away from Jimmy, a sobering reality set-in; Dalton didn't know what side of the collapse he was on, or what wall of the shaft he was actually feeling. Proceeding in the unobstructed direction could just as easily be leading him deeper into the mountain, either toward Ben Childress' corpse, or into the unexplored channel of the adit fork. He was playing a deadly lottery, his odds only one in three. A sense of dread returned to Dalton like the weight of a thousand cave-ins. He pondered his predicament. He couldn't be sure about Jimmy's injuries, and Jacob was still in trouble. There was no choice but to proceed. He moved on, keeping count of the support beams, calculating his distance from the exit.

At the twentieth wooden support set of Dalton's tally, it was time to make or break his method. If he were heading in the right direction, and if his count of the support-sets were correct, the end of the safety rope would be close by in the middle of the tunnel. What would happen now was beyond his control. Dalton swung his weapon to his back and dropped again to his hands and knees. To keep his orientation, he squared up his shoulders to the wall and crawled directly across the adit floor. If he couldn't find the rope, at least he'd find the opposite wall at the same depth; he'd have a chance to move further up the mine and try again without losing his bearings.

Dalton crawled slowly across the mine floor, pausing every few feet to lay flat on the ground and sweep his arms widely across the rock in search of the lifeline. Although he sensed he'd missed his target, his heart still dropped as he reached the opposite wall. His back-up system worked, however. He'd landed directly at the opposite vertical support. He'd maintained his calculated distance from the exit. He stood and moved a full stride along the wall, away from the cave-in. He assumed his knees again and moved across the mine in the fashion he'd made the first crossing. Still no luck.

Taking another long stride along the wall, Dalton turned and squatted. He started again across the adit floor. He slid to the middle of the shaft and laid flat, stretching out his arms until his shoulders felt as though they would dislocate. Panic began to set in as Dalton swept the floor. He floundered about, his clothes drenched from the damp rock and his own perspiration, his fingernails chipping and tearing as he scoured the rough floor for the rope. Nothing.

Once again, Dalton began to despair. *"The rope isn't here,"* he thought. *"I'm on the mountain side of the cave-in."* He laid his head on the ground and began to weep.

"No," Dalton screamed, suddenly, taking courage. *"They'll be coming for us,"* he thought, *"Jimmy reached 911. We left a note. We'll wait for them."*

As Dalton turned back toward Jimmy, his foot skidded over a protrusion. Unlike the hundreds of stones he'd grated over with his feet and knees since the cave-in, this object felt malleable. Dalton reached down to inspect the item. He felt the smooth texture of braided polyester, the safety-rope.

Dalton fell back to his knees. "Thank you, God, thank you," he cried.

Chapter 19

Seeing the Light

D alton shouted wildly down the adit, "I found it, Jimmy. I've got the safety-rope. I'll be back with help." With the rope in hand, he moved with relative ease. Pulling the line taut, he leaned back, using the resistance for guidance and balance. There was no longer a need to worry about counting support beams. The rope formed a straight line to the exit. He strode steadily along the lifeline in the darkness, keeping a grip, hand over hand.

Dalton sensed a sliver of light in the distance. His eyes were so immensely dilated it was impossible to focus, the intense sensation straining. He moved his eyes to the floor, relying on his peripheral vision. He was certain the glimmer ahead emanated from his cellar. As he neared the glowing beacon, Dalton lifted his gaze. Painful shards of light from the door pervaded his retinas like supernovas.

Fifty feet from the exit, Dalton heard what sounded like a faint whimper. He stopped and turned, trying to catch and decipher its source. Jimmy lay deep in the mine and the cry was unlike anything he had heard from Jacob. Dalton stood still, scanning the mine walls, listening. The void of the primitive drift-shaft stood next to him, its intense gloom contrasting the dimly lit main tunnel with gravity-like force.

Dalton turned back toward the cellar light that guided him. The blurred outline of the door was visible and the adit floor faintly illuminated. He dropped his safety-rope and ran toward home. As he burst through the door into his cellar, the note he'd posted slid loose from the screw and fluttered to the floor. He assumed his mom hadn't seen it. As he climbed the stairs to the kitchen, he heard her voice.

"Oh, there they are," Susan said into the phone. "They were in the cellar after all. We'll see you in a few minutes."

Dalton knew his mom had been speaking to a parent of one of his friends. Apparently, they were on their way over. He burst through the kitchen door with his rifle strapped across his back. His brown hair was matted with blood and soil. It hung from his brow in uneven strings, partially covering his eyes. Streams of dried blood emerged from his forehead and temples, accumulating in false scabs in the hair of his eyebrows and whiskers on his jawline. His exposed ears were black as coal, his left lobe split as though a piercing had been stripped out. The bridge of his nose was sliced horizontally to the bone, leaving a blood trail under each eye. His hands were coated with blood and dirt from the end of his long sleeves to his fingertips, each of his nails cracked and worn below the quick.

Susan stared at Dalton in a state bordering on clinical shock. His marred appearance provoked a memory of a black and white photograph she'd seen of her great-great-grandfather after a full day stoking flames on a coal train. Was it her son or a long-lost relative? She peered through Dalton's filthy bangs and spied his familiar boyish eyes. She rushed to her son, enveloping him in her arms. "What happened? What happened to you?" she cried. "You need a doctor."

Dalton reached for his mother's arms and tore himself loose. He stood in the kitchen in his filthy clothes, soaking wet from sweat and moisture from the mine. "I'm okay, Mom," he said. "Really. It's not as bad as it looks."

Immediately, the doorbell rang.

"Is it the Burrells, or the Irwins?" Dalton asked.

Susan looked at Dalton, confused. "The Burrells," she said. "Where's Jacob?"

Dalton propped his rifle behind the cellar door and moved to the foyer without answering his mother's question. Susan followed. He opened the front door. Their guests' reactions to his appearance were not unexpected.

"Where's Jacob?" Mrs. Burrell asked, frantically. "What happened to you?"

Jacob's parents had been nervous since their son failed to come home for his phone. Mr. Burrell eventually found Dalton's texts. It was his pleas for Jacob to come back over that prompted their phone calls and subsequent visit.

"We never saw him," Dalton explained. "That is, Jimmy and I." Dalton knew as anxious as the Burrells seemed, things were about to get much worse.

"I think Jacob's in trouble," he said plainly. "We heard him scream. Jacob and I found a body, Ben Childress."

Mrs. Burrell collapsed into her husband's arms. He guided her to a bench in the foyer as Dalton continued.

"Jimmy and I went looking for Jacob," Dalton said. "Now Jimmy's in trouble too, and I'm the only one who's not in the mine."

"Mine?" the three adults said, nearly in unison. The questions came fast and furious, peppered with fear and anger.

"Please stop," Dalton begged. "There'll be time for this later. We need to get help now. We need to find the sheriff. He knows there's a problem in the mine." He stepped outside to the landing as he spoke. The adults followed.

A full moon had risen above the valley's edge. Sheriff Buford was just pulling up. He spotted the conference and engaged his flashers as he parked near the Wallace residence.

Dalton described the exact course of events to the sheriff since Buford had been called away to the traffic accident in Ridgeway. The parents listened in horror. When he heard about the mine collapse, Mr. Burrell sprinted to the Irwin residence to get the trapped boy's parents. Buford reached into his cruiser and grabbed his handset. He asked the dispatcher to contact Denver about a mine extraction team. As Buford spoke on the radio, Susan Wallace called her husband in Utah. Dalton knew his dad would drive home immediately.

Another vehicle appeared on the pass above Lobos. Dalton could tell by its profile it was a large SUV. *"The reinforcements 911 promised Jimmy,"* he thought.

As the truck rounded the bend into town, Dalton was shocked to see it wasn't law enforcement at all. It was Cheyanne Connery's family, arriving from Querido. He quickly ran to meet Cheyanne as she and her parents exited the vehicle.

Cheyanne wrapped her arms around Dalton, ignoring the blood and grime that covered him. "What happened to you?" she said. "Are you okay? I saw your text. Why didn't you respond to me?"

"I'm so happy to see you," Dalton said. "Jimmy got trapped in a mine collapse while he and I were looking for Jacob. He's alive, but Jacob's still missing."

"And what about Ben?" Cheyanne asked. "You said —"

"—Yes," Dalton said, "I think we found his body. Jacob saw him."

Cheyanne's parents were listening in complete shock. Dalton led the Connerys over to the sheriff and Lobos parents as he filled in the details. Other townsfolk were gathering to see what was going on.

Jimmy Irwin's parents ran up to the crowd. Susan Wallace took them aside. She tried to delicately explain what Dalton had conveyed to them. Dalton saw their anguish and walked over to console and encourage them.

Buford finished up with dispatch and racked his radio. He chirped the cruiser's siren to get everyone's attention and grabbed his bullhorn. "Listen everyone," he said. "You all know the situation; Jimmy Irwin is trapped and injured in an abandoned mine. Jacob Burrell is missing and may or may not be in the same tunnel. Now then, there's an extraction team being put together in Denver. They'll be transported here via helicopter. We can expect them soon. In the meantime, no one is to enter the mine, and all questions need to be directed to me." The sheriff was covering all the bases, rising to the occasion. "Since we can't say for sure where Jacob is," he continued, "I'd like the adults to partner up and start searching around town. Parents, please take your children home. If you're by yourself, don't leave your kids unattended. Again, search only in pairs or groups."

Buford tossed the megaphone into the back seat of his cruiser and walked over to Dalton and his mom. The Irwins and Burrells followed, frantically asking questions of the sheriff. He gently raised his index finger indicating he'd be available shortly. Buford placed his hand on the small of Susan Wallace's back, leading her and Dalton away from the crowd. He explained to Susan that he needed Dalton to remain with him a while. He still had some questions. He asked that she take the Irwins and Burrells to Jimmy's house and wait for him there.

"What about Ben's mom?" Susan asked. "Has she been told?"

"She's staying with her folks in Montrose," the sheriff said. "We've sent somebody over."

The Connerys were anxious to help, to join the search. They approached the sheriff to see if their teenage daughter could go along with them.

"Probably not a good idea," Buford said. "You can leave her here with me and Dalton."

Cheyanne's parents agreed and dispersed with the others.

Buford walked Dalton and Cheyanne back to his vehicle, parked beneath a streetlight. He removed a pocketsize notebook from his vest, placing it on the hood of his car. The sheriff took a pen from his shirt pocket and asked Dalton to repeat the details of the day, leading up to his escape from the mine. Cheyanne grabbed Dalton's hand as she listened anxiously. The streetlight above was weak and its transparent cover filled with dead bugs; Buford struggled to read his notes. The sheriff asked Dalton if there was any other place Jacob might have gone. He specifically asked about the Winning Stakes Mine on the opposite side of the valley.

"Jimmy and I heard the scream from my cellar," Dalton said. "It couldn't have come from that far away."

Buford was undeterred and addressed Dalton and Cheyanne together. "I understand you sold a silver dollar to Horrance Taber," he said. "Where did it come from?"

The question left Dalton puzzled. "*What does that coin have to do with Jacob and Jimmy. With Ben Childress?*" he thought. Still, he was surprised Buford knew about their little transaction at the antique store. "We did sell a coin to Mr. Taber," he replied.

"Where did you get such a fine Morgan dollar?" the sheriff asked.

"It was a gift," Dalton said, using discretion he'd observed from Jacob.

"Well, it isn't nice to sell gifts," Buford said. The sheriff folded his notebook. He closed and slid it into his pocket. "I'm going to go check on Jimmy and Jacob's parents," he said. "Miss Connery, you hop in the squad car and lock yourself in. Dalton, go on home and wait for a medic. They're going to need to take a look at you."

Chapter 20

Through the Oval Lens

D alton grabbed his hunting rifle from the kitchen and took it upstairs, locking it in his safe. He moved to the front window of his bedroom to see Cheyanne in the cruiser below. The vehicle was quartered away so Dalton had a clear line of sight to the car's rear and passenger sides. He saw that the backseat of the car was empty. He strained to see inside the vehicle's forward compartment, but glare from the streetlight obstructed his view.

Dalton moved to the adjacent window casement in his room, eliminating the glare but complicating his perspective. He peered through the cruiser's back window toward the front of the car. The path was obscured by a gridded prisoner barrier, headrests, and various types of suspended equipment. Again, he couldn't see Cheyanne. He began to panic. *"I need to get closer."*

Under ordinary circumstances, using a telescopic device attached to a high-powered rifle to look for a human being would be considered crazy, but given the life-or-death environment thrust upon Dalton that night, he made that decision. He had no time to detach the scope from the gun. A town kid was dead, two of his friends' lives hung in the balance, and now Cheyanne, the most defenseless soul in his circle, was beyond the reach of his protection.

Dalton grabbed his rifle from the safe. The gun's shoulder-strap snagged a box of bullets as he pulled the weapon from his closet, scattering ammunition across the floor. He dropped the cartridge magazine from the rifle and locked open the firing chamber, assuring the weapon was unloaded and unable to discharge. He engaged the gun's safety-switch and assumed a firm stance, placing his eye behind the scope's oval lens. He raised the vision field in line with the rear window of the squad car.

The scope drew Dalton into the front compartment of the cruiser, penetrating the smallest openings between the car's seats and equipment. He was literally reading instrumentation on the dashboard, but there was no sign of Cheyanne. He spotted a cellphone sitting in the car's cupholder. He recognized its pink protective cover immediately. *"There's no way Cheyanne left that there,"* he thought. *"Maybe she's laying down across the seats."*

Using the scope's incredible magnification, Dalton squeezed through every open portal to the front compartment of the cruiser, but he couldn't see his friend. Unless Cheyanne was lying on the floor, she wasn't in the car.

Cheyanne couldn't understand why the sheriff had suddenly insisted she accompany him to an abandoned mining camp, halfway up a mountain. The trail was rocky and steep, and the shoes she wore were totally inadequate for hiking. Buford's interest in the mine seemed misguided, considering where Dalton had heard Jacob's scream.

As the sheriff lit their path with his tactical flashlight, he continued to pepper Cheyanne with questions about the source of the coin she and Dalton sold to Horrance Taber, "Young lady," he said, "I'm certain we're close to where you found that silver dollar. I'd like you to show me exactly where it happened."

Cheyanne was astounded by the question. "What does that coin have to do with finding Jacob Burrell or rescuing Jimmy Irwin?" she asked. "Or Ben Childress, for that matter."

"You do realize," the sheriff began, unfazed, "these mountains are riddled with mines. Many of them are connected."

Cheyanne couldn't get her head around what Buford was trying to say. "I'm not an expert," she said, "but I don't guess there are mines under the valley. We're on a completely different mountain."

"We can agree you're not an expert," the sheriff said.

Buford swapped his ruse without so much as a blush. "So, was Jacob with you when you found that coin up here?" he asked. "Or did you tell him where you found it? Maybe he came back by himself to look for more."

"As far as I know, Jacob doesn't know anything about the coin," Cheyanne answered, measuredly.

Buford was silent for several seconds. "Silver has a strange effect on people," he said, finally. "That missing boy, Ben Childress, bragged to some people about a silver coin he'd found. He told me he uncovered it near Gunnison. Maybe he's over there now, looking for it."

"Ben Childress' body is in the mine," Cheyanne said. "Dalton told you."

The further Buford and Cheyanne climbed above town, the more anxious Cheyanne became. Being alone with a stranger, even a lawman, went against everything she knew. "We're nowhere near where Dalton and I found that coin," she said. "It was close to the valley."

As they entered the Winning Stakes mining camp, Buford told Cheyanne to stop. "Now," he said, "we both know there's a hidden entrance into this mine complex, somewhere. Show me where it's at."

"Look," Cheyanne said, exasperated, "I told you we found the silver dollar near town, down in the valley. We were on a hike, and we followed a little stream. It was in a cave, not a mine."

D alton lowered his scope and observed the dimly lit street below his bedroom window. Cheyanne's family SUV was still parked just yards away, its windows left open in haste. He tried to imagine where Cheyanne might have gone. *"If she needed a bathroom, the sheriff would have brought her here,"* he reasoned. He raised his scope to the Sheriff's Annex and tiny business district of town. There was no sign of Sheriff Buford or Cheyanne.

Dalton scanned the yards and houses beyond the reach of the town's streetlights. Despite near-complete darkness, he was able to see clearly as the scope's optics gathered in the limited electrified light of the structures, and the moon's glow. He observed numerous people, pairs and small groups searching for Jacob, their paths intersecting and interweaving in the narrow valley. But what moments earlier had been a blessing for Dalton was now becoming a curse. The immense magnification of his scope was making his search tedious. Even at the scope's lowest setting, he was drawn in too close. He was searching square feet in an area measured in miles. He considered the numerous search parties and redundancy of effort. He turned his attention to more distant, more manageable targets on the edge of town.

Beginning with large yards in the town's peripheries, Dalton scanned unsearched territory. He meticulously combed fields and outbuildings of the neighboring acreages and ranchettes until he reached the valley's edge. He quickly saw the cave where he and Cheyanne had found the coins, the stream flowing gently toward the valley.

Dalton worked his way deeper into the wilderness. He slowly swept his oval vision field across a mental matrix of timbers, bluffs, and ravines he'd created on many summer hikes. Much of the lower regions of the mountain were heavily forested, impenetrable by the scope. He focused on the clearings, areas wiped clean by snow and rockslides. He scanned the lower third of the mountain. Other than a half dozen bighorn sheep, he'd seen no sign of life.

Halfway up the mountain, a giant field of uniform broken rock appeared in Dalton's lens. He recognized the tailings and debris below the Winning Stakes Mine.

B uford suddenly took hold of Cheyanne's arm and spun her around backward. He grabbed the hood of her sweatshirt, twisting it around his hand until he had a firm grip.

"What are you doing?" she screamed, struggling to break loose. Cheyanne's shoe slipped off as Buford brutally jerked her about. Jagged rocks stabbed at her exposed foot. She desperately tried to break away. "Leave me alone, freak," she cried.

Buford pulled Cheyanne back with ease. "Where do you think you're going?" he said. "Everything's going to be fine. We just need to keep walking until we find your little cave." With a firm grip on Cheyanne's sweatshirt, Buford marched the girl down a short ridge to a precipice high above the dimly lit town. "There's a good view from up here," he said. "Now, where is it?"

"I don't know where it is," Cheyanne said. "I'm not from around here."

"Is that right?" the Sheriff mocked. He was beginning to believe Cheyanne either couldn't remember or couldn't find the location she and Dalton found the silver coin.

Buford abruptly sweep-kicked Cheyanne's feet out from beneath her and swung her frame over the abyss.

"Help," Cheyanne cried in horror. Gravity pulled heavily on her body as Buford kept a tight grip on her hood. Only the sheriff's hold kept her from plunging to the valley floor.

The sheriff repeatedly pulled Cheyanne close to the ledge, only to release her again, making sure she knew the alternative he was offering. "It would be a shame if there were two accidents in Lobos today," he said.

"Oh, God," she screamed. Cheyanne swayed helplessly over the chasm. Her other shoe fell from her foot, disappearing into the valley. She grasped desperately for something to take hold of. A Bristlecone Pinetree jutted from the rock, mere feet away, but her reach fell short. She began to plead, "Please Sheriff," she said. "I'll help you. Let me try."

"You need to think really hard," Buford said. "We're running out of time."

Cheyanne inexplicably began to slide out of the bottom of her hoodie. She was falling despite Buford's hold. "No," she screamed. She instinctively locked her elbows to her side, pinning the sweatshirt under her arms, slowing her descent.

Buford swung Cheyanne's body violently back into the rock. Her hip banged brutally against the cliff's edge. Her frame hinged on the mountain rim.

Cheyanne locked eyes with Buford. It was understood between the two of them, the sheriff held total power over her life.

Buford moved his gaze to the town lights below. *"What to do with the little blabbermouth?"* he thought. *"She would have a story to tell. That would be messy."*

Cheyanne screamed a cry of the doomed.

Chapter 21

The Hardest Decision

C heyanne's harrowing scream pierced the black night, fracturing the still air and Dalton's hope for his friend's safety. Perched inside his open second-floor window, Dalton blindly jammed his index finger into the rifle's open firing chamber, making sure the gun was disabled. He could taste his sweat. Profuse drops of moisture ran from his brow, tracing the crease of his nose over the bow of his lip. That the cry came from Cheyanne was clear, but her location was still hidden. Dalton didn't know where to look. *"Stay within your system,"* he told himself. *"Work the grid."*

Through his scope, Dalton feverously combed the downhill edge of the mine clearing. Something strange appeared in the rim of his oval lens; a light-colored shoe stood out clearly on the ground, a woman's flat. He was certain it belonged to Cheyanne. He scoured the surrounding area looking for his friend, but there was no sign of her or the direction she'd gone. He observed the jagged rocks of the upper mining camp. *"Nobody's going up that way with a bare foot,"* he thought. *"She must have gone down."* But he had just searched that area.

Dalton was perplexed. He needed a new audible clue to home in on Cheyanne's location, but he dreaded what that might mean. A trail off the lower mine ruin led to the left, disappearing into dense trees. The path was cloaked in foliage. He moved his scope to the opposite side of the camp. An exposed ledge ran to the right, short but clear. The ridge quickly narrowed until its breadth was observable in his vision field. Dalton followed the outcrop toward its precipice and cliff. The dampness of his palms strained the grip on his rifle.

The force of Cheyanne's subsequent scream reached Dalton simultaneously with her image in his lens. She wasn't alone. A large man had a grip on her sweatshirt as she dangled above the abyss, Sheriff Buford. Her life literally hung in the balance.

Although Buford's grip seemed secure, he failed to pull Cheyanne up. Dalton considered that the sheriff wasn't strong enough. He thought of running to help. But something in Buford's posture was troubling. He didn't look at all taxed or distressed. He seemed relaxed, almost as if he were enjoying himself.

Dalton moved the scope's crosshairs to Cheyanne. Her lips frantically pulsed pleas for help as she flailed about. Buford effortlessly switched grip-hands. Clearly, he was not Cheyanne's savior. He was tormenting her.

In his young life, Dalton had never experienced how it felt to hate, to desire violence upon another. But his compulsion to act felt natural, instinctual. Endorphin-fueled rage surged within him, an urge to hurt, and to punish. He pulled away from his scope and looked into his closet. The spilled gun cartridges lay scattered across the wooden floor.

Lowering his rifle and propping it up against the windowsill, Dalton grabbed the empty ammunition clip at his feet and slid his opposite arm across the wooden floor, gathering three cartridges. He clicked the powerful ammunition into the magazine and snapped the assembly into his rifle. In a single motion, he brought the gunstock back to his shoulder, his eye before the scope. His movements were precise. The horrifying scene was once again clear through the oval lens.

Dalton placed the sight's crosshairs on the heart of Cheyanne's assailant. As he slowly exhaled, his body steadied, the lens-lines growing still. He had no doubt he could make the shot, but quickly realized his predicament: Separating Buford from his life would cut Cheyanne's only lifeline.

The sheriff clung tightly to Cheyanne, pondering his situation as he looked out across the valley on the moonlit ridge. Residential floodlights sparkled below as trees of the town bent with breezes, sifting their shine in and out of sight. Unintelligible murmurs from the townsfolk drifted up on delicate puffs of mountain air. The shifting of the sheriff's feet in the stone and gravel obscured their faint voices.

Buford again traded left hand for right on the girl's sweatshirt and reversed his footing, turning uphill toward the mine. The top rungs of the crumbling waterwheel shone clear in the moonlight, glancing over a stand of spruce saplings on a ridge. He visually traced the crest of the trees to the heart of the old mining camp. The stream that had powered the wheel ran snakelike between the ramshackle barracks of the camp and disappeared into the trees. The sound of running water resonated on the hillside, the delicate splatter of the creek tumbling over the rocks. Buford considered his trip to the camp on horseback, how he'd assumed he'd crossed the stream without knowing it. It was as if the creek had disappeared.

Cheyanne clung tightly to her hoodie with her arms. "I'm telling you Sheriff," she said, "We found the coins in a cave near the valley. A cave where a stream appears out of the mountain."

Buford looked below the camp to where he'd lost track of the creek. *"Maybe I've learned enough,"* he thought. *"That creek needs to be checked out on both ends."*

Sheriff Buford had made up his mind. There would be another *unfortunate accident* in Lobos that evening. "Young lady," he said, "in the future, you should be more careful while hiking at night."

"No," Cheyanne cried out, lunging for the Bristlecone Pine.

Buford saw Cheyanne's intention and pivoted her away from the tree, raking her petite frame along the jagged rock.

Desperate to find a handhold in the cliff face, Cheyanne released one arm from her side, perilously tilting her body above the abyss. She immediately began to slide out of her sweatshirt. She scraped a handful of sand from the sediment layers and launched the tiny projectiles at the sheriff, striking him in both eyes.

Buford heaved his head, blinking wildly. Cheyanne was swung about violently as the sheriff struggled to wipe the sand clear.

D alton pulled the bolt of his gun back, then pushed it forward, loading a cartridge into the firing chamber of his rifle.

S uddenly, the tree branch was within reach. Cheyanne latched on.

As Buford regained his senses, he realized his situation had grown more complicated. He stood resolute over his victim, pondering how to dislodge Cheyanne from the tree. Although she weighed less than a hundred pounds, the sheriff's arm grew tired. He gripped her sweatshirt with both hands, pulling with all his strength. The tree bowed against Buford's force.

Cheyanne's grip was loosening. Dalton could see she was losing her battle. He released the safety on his Browning rifle and quickly moved the crosshairs down Buford's torso to the large man's right thigh. He squeezed the trigger.

In the enhanced light of the scope, the matter exiting the back of Buford's leg appeared as pink vapor. Dalton observed the man fall to the ground. He nervously opened the gun's firing chamber and engaged the safety before swinging the scope back to the Bristlecone Pine. Cheyanne's image filled his oval lens. She climbed to safety through the tree's heavy limbs.

Dalton returned his sights to Buford and rearmed his weapon. He placed the scope's crosshairs squarely on the chest of the prone sheriff, looking for signs of aggression. He patiently held cover for Cheyanne as she climbed safely onto the ledge.

Chapter 22

Bonding Ties

In the faint light of the full moon, Cheyanne stood atop the ledge below the Winning Stakes Mine. Buford lay prone over a boulder, blocking the trail off the narrow precipice. The sheriff's right leg was severely damaged above the knee, his heavy respiration discernible in the stillness. Cheyanne moved cautiously toward the lawman, eyeing the service revolver strapped to his hip. She leaned over and picked up two stones; the larger of which she held in her throwing arm. She flipped the smaller stone in the sheriff's direction, looking for his reaction.

Buford didn't move.

Cheyanne bent down and carefully removed the sheriff's handgun from his holster. Pointing the weapon in Buford's direction, she strode over the thick man. Sharp stones carved at her bare feet as she moved off the ridge to the base of the mining camp. She stared down the considerable slope and distance to the dimly lit streets and yards below. She sat down in the jagged rubble, placing Buford's service revolver in the pocket of her stretched hoodie.

Dalton quickly stored his rifle in his closet safe and sprinted from his home. He crossed the narrow valley and climbed laser-like toward Cheyanne, bushwhacking up the mountain in the moonlight. He emerged at the mining camp, surprising Cheyanne, triggering a visceral response.

Cheyanne jumped to her feet, stone in hand.

"Easy," Dalton said in the darkness. "It's me."

Cheyanne dropped the stone and moved gingerly across the rugged trail toward Dalton, her eyes filling with tears.

Dalton ran to her, wrapping her tightly in his arms.

"He was going to kill me, Dalton," Cheyanne said, laying her cheek on Dalton's chest, her head nestled beneath his chin.

"I know," he said.

"The sheriff's been shot," Cheyanne continued. "But I think he's alive. I grabbed his gun." She pulled back slightly from Dalton, nodding in the direction of Buford. She drew the pistol from her pocket and guided Dalton's hand to the barrel's cold steel.

Dalton confirmed the pistol was disabled and pushed it back into Cheyanne's pocket. He gazed down the narrow ledge toward the injured sheriff. Buford's tactical flashlight shimmered in a bush near the fallen man. "We can use that light," he said. "Wait here." He hustled out the ridge by the light of the moon.

Dalton grabbed Buford's flashlight and attended to the sheriff. The lawman lay unconscious, blood flowing steadily from his leg. Dalton removed his own belt and strapped a tourniquet tightly around Buford's upper thigh. The bleeding immediately subsided. He checked the sheriff's pulse and breathing before patting him down for additional weapons. Satisfied the man was stable and harmless, Dalton left the sheriff for medics and legitimate authorities.

"He's not going anywhere," Dalton said, as he returned to Cheyanne's side.

Cheyanne grabbed onto Dalton. "Is he dead?" she said.

"No," Dalton replied. "Hopefully, he'll live a long life in prison. But he'll have a limp."

At last, Cheyanne questioned where the shot had come from, who had saved her. The sound of the supersonic blast had been crystal clear, trailing the bullet's impact by more than a second. She recognized it was a long shot. "Who else is up here?" she asked. "Who shot Buford?"

"It was me," Dalton said. "From my room. I took a chance going for the leg."

Cheyanne pulled Dalton in close. The couple held on to one another with age-old instincts. In that instant, Dalton felt he knew his purpose in the world.

Dalton took Cheyanne's hand and guided her slowly off the mountain, his oversized shoes flopping about on her feet. As they entered the glowing veil of streetlights in town, they heard a growing murmur of an approaching crowd. Remarkably, Buford's cruiser remained the only law enforcement vehicle in sight.

As the couple waited conspicuously under the streetlight for the excited hordes, Dalton moved to Cheyanne and wrapped his arms around her waist.

Even in the dim light, Cheyanne's green eyes sparkled like the stars. Dalton was drawn in like the carbon within him returning to the heavens.

Cheyanne placed her arms around Dalton's neck, her wrists crossed relaxed behind his head. She no longer saw the personable, attractive boy she'd come to know. Rather, a principled man of action, someone willing to take risks for what was right, for what he loved. She pulled herself in close and kissed Dalton's parched and bruised lips.

Dalton had never felt anything so wonderful.

As the sound of the excited adult voices grew louder, Dalton suddenly jerked away.

"What is it?" Cheyanne said, startled.

"I have to go back into the mine; I have to help Jimmy," he said. "I'm sure Jacob's there too."

"I'm going with you!" Cheyanne said.

"I want that," Dalton said, lying. "But I need you to tell the adults about Buford, tell my parents where I am." He felt the pistol in Cheyanne's sweatshirt pocket. "Do you know how to use this?" he said.

"Of course, but I thought this was over," Cheyanne said, "Buford's done."

"It won't be over, until we have Jacob and Jimmy back," Dalton said. "Promise me you'll stay here until your parents get back."

"Promise," she said.

Dalton helped Cheyanne into her family's truck. He leaned in, kissing her. "See you in a minute," he said. He slammed the door shut and ran toward his house.

Chapter 23

Going it Alone

D alton tramped down into his cellar and switched on Buford's tactical flashlight. Even in the well-lit room, he could see its strong beam. He turned to the moving boxes to look for batteries, wanting back-up. The partially emptied package of D-cells that failed him on the last trip lay open on top of the pile. He pinched the clamshell pack closed. "Dead bunnies," he said, launching the package blindly toward a garbage can on the opposite side of the room. Determined not to get caught in the dark again, he grabbed a second, larger pack of batteries, stripped it open, and crammed its contents into his pockets.

Dalton looked for tools to free Jimmy; a shovel, anything to move debris or gain leverage. He spotted a prybar, a three-foot iron rod, shaped like a cane. When he was younger, he'd seen an auto-tech peal a car tire off a rim with one. *"That should do it,"* he thought.

Finally, Dalton picked up his Browning rifle. He inserted a loaded magazine, opened the firing chamber, and set the safety. He slung the weapon across his back and entered the mine. He traversed the first fifty feet of the tunnel without regard to the guide rope or support beams. He'd grown familiar with the upper echelons of the main shaft and knew he wouldn't easily get lost. Sixty feet in, he stopped and called out Jimmy's name, but there was no response.

Dalton continued down the adit, flashlight in one hand, prybar in the other. The shuffling of his boots and swish of his blue jeans produced a clamor in the stillness. Even with Buford's powerful tactical flashlight at his side, the solitude and darkness of the mine produced an eeriness Dalton hadn't experienced going in with a partner.

A faint but clearly human sound immediately found Dalton's ears. "*Jimmy*," he thought. "I'm coming, buddy," he shouted down the mine as he picked up the pace.

Another, much louder cry, stopped Dalton cold, its echo seeming to fall upon him from all sides. "Hang tight, Jimmy," he screamed, "I'm coming."

A third wail rang out in the mine, instinctively spinning Dalton backward in the direction of the sound. He lost his balance on the uneven floor and tripped over the rubble, somersaulting backwards to a jarring stop against the rock wall.

Virtually the entire town of Lobos had gathered in Breitling's parking lot where the Connerys had also migrated. Cheyanne sat sandwiched between her parents in the back seat of their SUV. Her mom and dad conversed about the horrifying events in Lobos that day, pausing occasionally to embrace their daughter. Mr. Connery complained about the time it was taking for the authorities to arrive; nearly twenty minutes had passed since they'd called 911.

Cheyanne stared intently up the street at the Wallace residence's closed front door, the last place she'd seen Dalton before he disappeared into the mine. The fact that he was still alone inside the shaft was inconceivable, but her pleas to follow, alone or as a group, had been immediately shut down. She endured her parents' doting hugs and condolences, thinking only of her friend and the insufferable lack of support he was getting.

Lights of emergency vehicles streamed over the pass and the air was suddenly filled with the thump of helicopter blades. A chopper circled town, scanning the landscape by spotlight for a clearing. The pilot effortlessly sat the machine down in the implement lot behind Breitling's Grocery. Spectators gathered around the helicopter to watch the mine extraction team unload. Susan Wallace stood by, ready to lead the rescuers to her home and down to the mine entrance.

"*Finally*," Cheyanne thought.

As the team methodically unloaded their gear from the choppers, vehicles from the state patrol, sheriff, and county fire-and-rescue departments queued up on Main Street. The first responders exited their trucks, waiting for instructions. Parents and townsfolks rushed upon them, shouting questions. It wasn't clear who was in charge.

"This is madness," Cheyanne said.

At last, the Connerys spotted Susan Wallace speaking with a team of supervisors. Cheyanne's parents climbed out of their SUV to join them, instructing their daughter to stay put.

W reathing in pain from the fall, Dalton rolled to his knees and reached for his flashlight. Pain racked his back from his right shoulder to his left hip, the pattern of the rifle strapped across his back. The gun barrel had taken the brunt of impact as he tumbled backward, distributing the misery along its form. A secondary sting, a pain like fire, scorched the back of Dalton's head. He ran his trembling fingers over the wound. He didn't need light to know the slippery dampness was blood. The rock wall had inflicted a large gash in his skull. He applied pressure with his hand, trying to stop the bleeding.

A faint, muffled voice echoed up the adit. *"Jimmy's stable again,"* Dalton thought. He pondered the inconsistency of the cries. The call that had spun him around had been much louder and seemed to echo off the walls behind him.

The ebbs of pain in Dalton's back waned, but his head was another matter. The sharp sting evolved to a slow throbbing pulse, spreading over the top of his scalp, collecting behind his eyes. He lifted his gun strap over his head and brought the weapon before him. The gun stock was cracked and there was an obvious bend in the barrel. His prized Browning was ruined. The oval lens of his unique scope was shattered. Discarding the rifle, Dalton picked up the prybar and found his feet.

A dynamic cry pierced the silence. This one clearly came from behind Dalton. No additional calculations were necessary. The only anomaly between him and the exit was the primitive drift, the side-shaft, fifty feet in. *"It's Jacob."* he thought.

Dalton swiftly backtracked up the mine, hollering over his shoulder, "Jimmy, I'll be back. I found Jacob."

Chapter 24

Deadly Curious

C heyanne watched as the mine extraction team busily organized their gear in the Wallaces' front yard. Vehicles from nearly every state emergency agency lined the street. The beefy construction of the Connerys' SUV eerily muffled the sound of the intense action taking place all around her. Cheyanne saw her mom and dad speaking with a state trooper in a field between Dalton's house and the business district. Light fog was beginning to form in the valley.

A lone set of headlights emerged on the pass above town. Cheyanne observed them repeatedly vanish and reappear as they descended the highway switchbacks to the valley floor. The vehicle entered the low light of the town center and parked on a side street near Breitling's Grocery. She could see the car was a late model mini-van. The make and model of the vehicle were familiar to Cheyanne, though the fog obscured its color. "*Jacob's parents have a car like that*," she thought.

A baseball hat-cladded figure exited the van and disappeared between two buildings. Cheyanne looked back at the Wallace residence. The yard and street were nearly empty now. She sighed in relief. "*They're on their way down to Dalton, Jimmy, and Jacob*," she thought. "*Unless . . . Unless, Jacob's not in the mine.*" She exited the vehicle and cautiously followed the character between the downtown buildings.

D alton entered the primitive tunnel where he'd heard Jacob's cry. What existed for wooden braces were badly disintegrated and the shaft appeared unstable. The drift was a fraction of the size of the main adit shaft.

With each yard traversed, the tunnel seemed to narrow. Dalton was forced to his hands and knees. His sides and aching back grazed and bumped protruding rocks as he crawled deeper into the void. Each knee-step induced a new and intense pain. Dalton shined his light into the distance. A fallen ceiling support lay wedged diagonally across the center of the drift. *"That's gonna be tight,"* he thought.

Even before he reached the new obstacle, Dalton started to stress over the narrow confines of the tunnel. As a kid, he'd purposely put himself in similar confinements for fun, lodging himself underneath or between various pieces of furniture or appliances in his home where an involuntary impulse to escape would kick-in. In those days, there was no genuine danger. This was real. Dalton was suddenly overwhelmed with panic. His heart began to race like wingbeats of a hummingbird, and heat flowed through his veins like threads on fire.

Suddenly, a scream unlike any Dalton had heard rang out in the mine. It was Jacob, and he was close by. Dalton focused laser-like down the tunnel. The shock of the cry shrouded his anxiety about the confined space. He surged forward along the mine floor, forgetting his insecurity, oblivious to the agonies wrought out by the hard and cramped space.

Dalton reached the blockage in the tunnel. His trepidation about the fallen obstruction had been wholly warranted. Although the collapsed support beam didn't appear to affect the integrity of the mine, it was firmly wedged in his path. He hammered on the wooden support with his crowbar, but the tool simply bounced off. He tried prying under the timber, but the thing was jammed into the tunnel floor. He would have to contort his frame and squeeze past the brace; a space half as wide as what he'd already been struggling with in the drift.

Once again, anxiety overcame Dalton like the weight of a summer squall. He dimmed his light and closed his eyes, trying to gather himself. He peered into his psyche, desperately seeking calm from within. The mental space he found was indistinguishable from the cave, spatially confined, yet boundless in capacity for fear. He lay motionless, hand across his chest, his heart pounding distress signals through his ribs.

Dalton's index finger glanced across a hard protrusion between his clavicles, the cross he wore around his neck. *"Jacob,"* he thought, finally, opening his eyes. He screamed down the tunnel for his friend. There was no response. He took hold of the flashlight and crowbar, but before he could switch on the lamp, he saw a flicker of light down the tunnel. "I'm coming," he screamed into the void.

Dalton inched forward to the fallen brace. The gap on either side of the obstacle was less than a foot wide. He slid the flashlight and prybar into his belt and reached forward, grabbing hold of the fallen timber with both hands. He rolled to his side, pressing his sore back tightly to the tunnel wall. Like a horizontal pullup, he pulled himself forward until his chin was even with the old timber. Running out of leverage, he released the brace and stretched his arms further down the mine. Grasping and scraping for handholds with his fingers and toes, he squeezed his torso between the fallen timber and stone. As his chest and stomach cleared the barrier, his thighs slid behind the brace. Without his legs for leverage, Dalton relied completely on his arms. Locating one grippable rock at a time, he dragged his body along the rock wall until he came clear. "Thank you," he shouted into the void.

As quickly as Dalton's exuberance arose, it was quashed. He realized the prybar had slid out of his belt. It lay several feet behind the brace. Retrieving it would mean two more passes through the bottleneck. "*Jacob can't wait,*" he thought. "*We'll need the tool to free Jimmy. Jacob and I will pick it up on the way back.*"

Dalton quickly covered several yards down the tunnel. He rested briefly and turned off his flashlight, looking for the light he'd seen. A solid glow lay directly ahead, its intensity suggesting his goal was near. He re-engaged his flashlight and crawled onward. Within minutes, the end of the drift shaft was in view. Dalton realized the illumination he'd seen was not the source of light at all, rather, the radiation of something bigger, something hidden behind a door. He'd found a passage similar to the one in his own cellar. A stray stream of light bled through a crack near its hinges. He crept silently toward the door.

Dalton peered through the fissure in the passage, an acute angle limiting his perspective. A single lightbulb hung from a crudely-wired fixture on the ceiling of a simple rock-walled space. A view to the lower half of the room was obstructed. He closed his eyes and lowered his body to the tunnel floor, listening for signs of life. The sound of faint human voices permeated the passage, two people conversing. One of them was Jacob.

Chapter 25

Alternate Route

C heyanne walked into the small downtown area to where she calculated the driver of the familiar vehicle left the street. A narrow alley diverged from the sidewalk, separating a pair of nineteenth-century buildings, their stone foundations merging into the rock from which they were hewn. The two-story buildings and ascending mountain configured an intimidating dead-end out of the alleyway. She called out Jacob's name as she nervously edged her way in.

A draped window on Cheyanne's left filtered the only visible light in the passage, its subtle radiance illuminating the dark continuous facade of the opposing building. She inched in closer. The glowing window was situated in the upper half of a narrow wooden door. A gap in the window drapes revealed a landing area, connected alternately to a kitchen and a staircase. A low-voltage light glowed above the foyer. An open refrigerator suggested the kitchen was no longer in use, the appliances and furniture appearing to derive from a time closer to the house's origin than the present day.

Cheyanne gazed through the kitchen towards a connected dining room. A baseball cap sat atop a table. She knocked on the door, but no one answered, no lights clicked on. She opened the door and allowed herself in. In front of her, stairs led down to a cellar, two flights configured in a right angle, separated by a landing.

"Jacob," she called out.

D alton lay breathless in front of the tunnel passage. A man's stern voice permeated the mineshaft, his words unclear. A responding, distressed utterance followed. It was Jacob, and he was in trouble. Dalton realized his cries for Jacob had destroyed all pretense to a surprise entry. He looked down at the heavy flashlight in his grasp. His hands trembled in fear. There were no other options; he lunged at the mine door, propelling his weight into the wooden structure with the leverage he could manage in the cramped space. The latch gave way and he summersaulted in on his hands and knees. He sprung to his feet clutching his flashlight, anticipating a fight.

Dalton found himself in a deserted, dirt-floored room. Only a few cardboard boxes lined the walls. An open doorway stood opposite the mine door. There was no place to hide in the sparsely-filled space. He instinctively moved behind the entryway wall opposite the mine door to conceal himself. The air was heavy with humidity and reeked of mold. He stood motionless, desperate to control the sound of his breathing. Minutes passed, but no one came. He crept toward the adjoining room. It appeared uninhabited, but there was no way to see directly behind the wall. He raised his heavy flashlight defensively and strode into the room.

A man's voice called out behind Dalton, spinning him around.

"Welcome," the man said.

Horrance Taber stood behind Jacob, resting a knife on the young man's throat. The shopkeeper wore a thin coat extending to his knees. A line of buttons strung from his thighs to his neck, the top fastener clasped tightly below his Adam's apple. The garment's white shoulders betrayed its original color, the front and sleeves opaquely stained by dark unidentifiable grime. His grey polyester trousers draped below the dirty coat, forming loose sheaths around black rubber boots. His pale face displayed its characteristic stubble beneath bland emotionless eyes. Muscular knots of his powerful forearms alternately poked beneath the jacket's cuffs.

Jacob was seated, his arms bound behind his back, his feet duct-taped to chair legs. His long-sleeved tee-shirt and jeans were dark with sweat. The shirt's elastic collar sagged between his clavicles under the weight of his perspiration, his brown leather belt stretched and stained. Streams of moisture darkened his soiled blond hair and flowed beneath his brow, streaking his dirty face, his dark eyes deadened.

Dalton looked at Taber. "What are you doing?" he screamed. He took a stride in the man's direction.

Taber pressed his knife against Jacob's neck.

Jacob felt the sting of the blade and burn of his own salty perspiration in the wound. "No, Dalton," he said, straining to scream, each word working Taber's knife deeper into his flesh.

"That's right, Jacob," Taber said. "Tell your friend."

The man in front of Dalton was nearly unrecognizable from the meek shopkeeper he'd met. Convinced Taber had either gone insane or was on drugs, Dalton searched for an angle to pull rationality from the man. "Mr. Taber," he began, "Jacob hasn't done anything to you. Let us help you."

"I'll be fine," Tabor mused. "As long as I fulfill my obligations to the powers that be."

Dalton considered whether Taber was referring to civil jurisdictions or some dark, mystical authority.

"Ultimately, we only answer to God, Mr. Taber," Dalton said.

"Tell that to the sheriff," Taber muttered.

Dalton saw his polite overture was going nowhere and stepped toward the pathetic character.

"No, Dalton," Jacob screamed.

C heyanne froze in fear at the sound of Jacob's hidden cry. "*Why is he calling for Dalton?*" she thought. An otherwise unintelligible conversation resonated below. Along with Jacob, Cheyanne heard the forbidding voice of an unfamiliar adult male. She started cautiously toward the stairs but spotted the casing's open railings. A single step could expose her to the area below. She dropped to her knees and quickly tied her hair in a knot. She placed her hands on the floor. Leaning out and down, she lowered her eyes below the basement ceiling. A production of indiscernible shadows played out on the dirt floor, silhouettes from an adjoining room.

Cheyanne stood and crept down the first flight of stairs to the elevated landing. A shelf suspended from the basement ceiling obscured her view. She separated a pair of boxes on the ledge and peered between them. It was clear she could reach the cellar floor without being noticed but breaching the doorway to the adjoining room was certain to give her away. She observed how the hanging shelf in front of her spanned the ceiling from room to room, its supports fastened firmly to the joists above. She pulled her petite frame atop the ledge and quietly navigated her way between the boxes and rubbish.

T aber slid a second chair next to Jacob's. "Take a seat," he instructed Dalton. "And leave the flashlight on the floor."

When Dalton hesitated, Taber again pushed his blade against Jacob's throat. Blood ran freely down the young man's neck, splitting his clavicles. Jacob whimpered, unable to speak or breathe.

"Stop," Dalton said. "I'll do it." He dropped his flashlight and raised his hands in surrender. He moved slowly toward the empty chair.

Jacob gasped for breath as Taber lightened the pressure on his airway.

Dalton sat down and Taber moved in quickly behind him, positioning the point of his knife firmly between Dalton's shoulder blades.

"Now," Taber demanded, "Hands behind you." He pried the end of a duct-tape strip from its roll using his teeth, keeping the sharp tip of his weapon on Dalton's back. He twisted the spool with his free hand, wrapping Dalton's wrists. Taber kicked at his victim's feet, directing them to the chair legs. He wrapped Dalton's ankles as he had his arms. He sheathed his knife and moved in front of Dalton. "Not so tough without your flashlight, are you?" Tabor taunted.

Dalton tested the bindings, flexing his arms and legs. The tape tore at the hair of his limbs. He wasn't moving. He looked over at his friend. Jacob's condition was worsening, his head slumped forward to his chest. Dalton moved his stare to Taber, his eyes blazing with rage. "You're a sick man," he said. "A freakish deranged maniac."

Tabor ignored Dalton's insults, turning his gaze toward Jacob. A sadistic grin formed on the grizzly man's pale face.

A s Cheyanne drew closer to the adjoining room, a third voice became clear. It belonged to Dalton. Terrified, she labored to move faster. The path was blocked by double-stacked paint cans and junk of every sort. One by one, she lifted the articles, placing them behind her, quietly sliding her body forward, taking their place.

A motion near the ceiling caught Dalton's eye. Cheyanne was staring at him from a suspended shelf.

Locking eyes with Dalton, Cheyanne raised her index finger to her lips, signaling silence. From her cramped perch, she observed Dalton strapped to the chair, Jacob slumped over at his side. The sight of her friends' peril fanned flames of rage within her. She reached into the pocket of her sweatshirt, sliding her hand over the handle of Buford's service weapon. She ran her index finger down the barrel of the steel, millimeters from the trigger. Using her free hand, she grabbed a ceiling joist and pulled herself forward a final increment.

Taber stepped in front of Jacob, grabbing a handful of his hair, pushing his head back, exposing his neck. "Here we go," he said. He spoke as if making a proclamation. He positioned the tip of his blade under Jacob's ear.

A suspended iron waterpipe ran parallel to the shelf next to Cheyanne. She grabbed hold and swung from the rafters, hinging her kicking leg, striking Taber flush in the face with her knee.

Taber spilled backward and lay motionless as Cheyanne dropped to the floor. She quickly pulled Buford's service revolver from her sweatshirt, pointing the weapon at the prone shopkeeper. She grabbed Taber's knife and cut the duct-tape restraining Jacob. She inspected the superficial abrasions on his neck.

Jacob stood gingerly and tried to tear the bindings from Dalton's arms and legs. Cheyanne gently moved him aside, finishing the job with Taber's blade.

Dalton and Jacob lifted Taber from the floor, placing him in the seat that had been Dalton's. They pinned Taber to the chair as Cheyanne firmly bound him.

Chapter 26

Leave No Man Behind

Dalton, Cheyanne, and Jacob walked slowly down the street, the latter draped between his friends' shoulders, all three oblivious to the state troopers rushing into Taber's antique shop.

"You guys are nuts," Jacob said. "Where did you even come from, Dalton?"

"The first side-shaft in the mine behind my house, fifty feet in," Dalton said. "It led directly to Taber's cellar. It's sad, but I think that's how he was getting rid of bodies, Ben Childress, until the shaft collapsed."

"Collapsed?" Cheyanne said. "How did you get through?"

"With great difficulty," Dalton said, smiling.

"You said, bodies," Cheyanne said. "Who else did Taber kill?"

"Hard to say," Dalton said. "But I'm willing to bet Taber is the killer from twenty years ago, over in Durango. He probably pleaded down on a single count and got out on probation. I'll be shocked if Taber is even his real name."

"Obviously, you didn't listen to Buford either," Jacob said, addressing Dalton. ". . . about staying in your house. What's he going to say about all this?"

"There's something else, Jacob," Dalton said. "Buford got shot. He was a real bad guy."

"Dead?" Jacob asked.

Dalton shook his head. "No, but he tried to kill Cheyanne, it was the Browning that took him down."

"Wow," Jacob said, recognizing the implication for his friend.

"Anyway," Dalton continued, "Buford was only interested in silver. He thought there was a pile of it stashed up here, stolen in a home invasion years ago in Denver."

"I remember that," Jacob said. "I was like, ten."

Cheyanne spoke up. "Buford told me Ben Childress found some silver near Gunnison, then sent him on a wild goose chase."

"That fits," Dalton said. "Buford told Jacob and me he thought Ben had gone inside the Winning Stakes Mine. He must have interrogated Ben. Then arranged a *chance meeting* with Taber."

Jacob looked at Dalton pensively. "So, Buford brought Taber in on purpose—as a fall guy."

"Maybe. Or to clean-up loose ends," Dalton said.

"Like Ben," Cheyanne said, the corners of her lips sinking.

"And maybe you and me, had things gone differently," Dalton said. "But circumstances gave Buford a chance to handle you, himself."

"Why the two of you, though?" Jacob asked. "Why me?"

"Because Cheyanne and I found a few silver dollars in a cave below the Winning Stakes Mine the other day. We sold one to Taber. Buford must have heard about it and assumed it was part of the stolen treasure. He tried to get information from us."

Cheyanne's eyes brightened. "So, that's why the sheriff was grilling me about the coin, the mine."

"But that doesn't explain me," Jacob said. "Buford had no reason to believe I was a threat to his plan. Apart from being friends with the two of you."

Dalton considered how his best friend came to his dire circumstance. "How did Taber nab you, anyway?" he said.

"On my way back to your house," Jacob replied. "He was on the street—said you were at his place. He followed me in and knocked me on the head. I woke up in the chair."

Dalton reached behind Jacob's head. A walnut-sized mound disjointed his close-cropped hair. "Buford may have thought we told you something," he said. "Set you up, like Ben. Or maybe you were just an opportunity the old psychopath couldn't pass up."

A commotion broke out in front of Dalton's house. Jimmy Irwin was being brought out on a stretcher. The three teens rushed to his side.

"We were about to come and get you," Dalton said wryly.

Jimmy mustered a smile. The paramedics were about to load him into the ambulance when he inexplicably sat up. He reached into his pocket and pulled out Dalton's handgun. The medics took a step backward.

"I found this while I was waiting—," Jimmy said. "I had plenty of time."

Dalton smiled, taking the gun. He opened its cylinder and dropped its five cartridges into his hand. He slid the revolver and bullets into his pockets.

"Thanks buddy," Dalton said. "Thanks for hanging in there. You'll have a heck of a good story to write at Dartmouth."

"Or Yale," Jimmy said, smiling.

Jimmy's medical transport sped away as the three remaining friends looked on. Throngs of townsfolk, reporters, paramedics and police encircled them.

"It looks like we all have a few appointments," Dalton said. "Jacob, you're next for an ambulance."

Jacob pulled Dalton in close, his arm still draped across his friend's shoulder. "Let me get this straight," he whispered. "You found silver dollars in a cave and didn't tell me about it?"

"It's called discretion, Jacob," Dalton replied. "You should know, I learned it from you."

Dalton looked into Jacob's eyes, wondering what was going through his head. When his friend had suffered enough, he offered the truth. "Actually," he said, "I forgot to tell you. I might have been distracted by a certain green-eyed girl."

"That's acceptable then," Jacob said, smiling. "You can show me your secret spot when this all clears up."

Paramedics led Jacob to an ambulance as Dalton turned to Cheyanne. The young couple stood face to face, holding one another's hands, eyes locked in a knowing moment. Cheyanne moved in close, wrapping her arms tightly around Dalton's neck. She kissed him softly on the lips.

Dalton saw Cheyanne's parents rushing toward them. "Here come your folks," he said. "Tell them not to hate me."

"Oh, shit," she said. "It's me they're going to kill. I'll probably be grounded for like, I don't know, forever."

"I guess our date with Taber's money's gonna have to wait," Dalton said.

"Well, at least we'll see each other in school," Cheyanne said. "Sit with me on the bus?"

Dalton smiled.

As Cheyanne's parents led her away, Dalton could see the eastern horizon brightening at the edge of the valley. He turned toward his house, looking for his parents.

Chapter 27

Unconditional

Steve drafted the police cruiser at speeds that under other circumstances would have cost him a bundle. The trooper had escorted him from the Utah state line. They made the trip in half the normal time.

Susan met her husband as he exited his car. She threw her arms around him.

"Where is he?" Steve said, clinging to his wife.

Dalton appeared behind his father. "I'm so sorry that I went into the mine," he said. "That I broke the rules."

Steve grabbed his son, consuming him in a hug. "Thank God," he said.

Susan pried her way in and the three embraced, both parents sobbing silently.

Dalton finally broke the huddle. "It won't happen again," he said.

"There's time to discuss it later," Steve said. "You were protecting your friends, that's the important thing."

Medics collected Dalton and began their triage. The Regional Commander of the state police stood by with several other officers, waiting to take his statement.

Dalton walked into his house and went upstairs for a shower, feeling more like a man than when he'd woken up the previous day. As he undressed, he pulled his silver chain and its precious pendant over his head, laying it on his nightstand. As the shower's warm water washed away his dried blood, he rehashed the day's events, pondering the indelible marks left on his soul, new and old.

With his pistol cleaned and stored securely in its safe, Dalton climbed into bed. Outside, helicopter blades pounded the morning air as the rescue team prepared for its return to Denver. But in Dalton's heart there was peace. He laid his head on his pillow and slept.

www.ingramcontent.com/pod-product-compliance
Lightning Source LLC
Chambersburg PA
CBHW060438130626

46555CB00005B/2411